A Different Approach and Other Stories

Alex Grant

Copyright © Alex Grant 2025

All Rights Reserved

No part of this publication may be reproduced, distributed, or transmitted in any form or by any means, including photocopying, recording, or other electronic or mechanical methods, without the author's prior written permission, except in the case of brief quotations embodied in critical reviews and certain other non-commercial uses permitted by copyright law. For permission requests, please get in touch with the author.

Disclaimer:

All characters in the book are purely fictional and any resemblance to real persons living or dead is purely coincidental

Contents

DEDICATIONS I

ACKNOWLEDGEMENTS II

TAPP 1

A DIFFERENT APPROACH 28

THE VERY TERRIBLE THING 49

WHERE DOES ANYTHING START? 55

AN IMPORTANT MEETING 73

QUESTIONS 87

LUCKY MONDAY 98

MY UNCLE ROY 108

BE CAREFUL WHAT YOU WISH FOR 127

THE STARTLING CONCLUSIONS THAT WERE REACHED AFTER THE FIRST DAY'S QUESTIONING 136

Dedications

To everyone who's ever inspired me through their literature, music, or behaviour. And to my sons who, on being given each story to read after I'd written it, inevitably replied with something like, "It's good, but it's weird."

Acknowledgements

When The Ramones were inducted into the Rock and Roll Hall of Fame in 2002, Dee Dee said. "Hi, I'm Dee Dee Ramone, and I'd like to congratulate myself, and thank myself, and give myself a big pat on the back. Thank you, Dee Dee. You're very wonderful. I love you".

Ditto.

TAPP

"...let the punishment fit the crime, the punishment fit the crime." Gilbert and Sullivan. The Mikado

It was the morning of Wednesday 22nd March, and Mason Torville was very nearly dead. He had at most twenty-four hours to live—probably rather less than that, in Keith Hayman's opinion—and Keith was a very good judge of this sort of situation.

Torville looked awful—unsurprisingly. He had been strapped to a bed since the start of his sentence, which was now in its fourth day. He mumbled something as Keith walked into his cell, but whatever it was, it wasn't clear. It certainly wasn't a repetition of "fuck you" or "please don't", both of which he had, respectively, spat out and then pleaded on the first day. Whatever it was, Keith ignored it anyway. He always did. He guessed Torville's brain might not even be registering what was going to happen.

Keith, however, knew exactly what was going to happen. He was going to follow The Authorised Punishment Plan (usually abbreviated to TAPP).

He approached the bed, grabbed Torville's lower jaw, and with his left hand yanked it sharply downwards. Keith was no longer worried about being bitten, but nevertheless he wore the regulation protective gloves. With his right hand, he picked up a jug containing heavily salted water and poured some of it into the open mouth. Torville coughed and half-vomited, but Keith methodically kept a stop-and-start pouring action until all the liquid had gone. He knew that it hadn't all—or perhaps even mostly—been swallowed. That didn't matter. Some of it had. He had followed TAPP.

Presumably, Torville's brain was simultaneously telling him to drink the water because he was so dehydrated and telling him not to because it was so unpleasant and would actually only make matters worse.

As soon as that was done, Keith placed the jug on the small trolley he had entered the room with and picked up the baseball bat, which had also been on the trolley. He raised it head high, took careful aim, and brought it down solidly onto the area around Torville's right shin. He was almost certain that something was already broken down there after what he had done yesterday, but he was doing what TAPP required him to do. There was a loud moan rather than a scream.

Next came three heavy blows to the rib and chest area with the bat, and finally one to the head. There wasn't even a moan this time—more a sort of barely audible and despairing gasp.

Yeah, one more day at most, Keith thought, leaving the cell with the trolley and dropping his protective gloves into the bin outside the cell.

Now he had to do the admin.

Walking into the office he shared with Patrick Osobo, he sat down at his computer and confirmed that what he had just done exactly matched the requirements of the sentence.

'Doctor to be on standby for certificate signing from 6 p.m. on 22nd March,' he added in the ETOD (Estimated Time Of Death) section of the document.

Under 'Additional Comments', he noted that Torville's cell smelled very strongly indeed of 'bodily discharges'. That wasn't exactly rare given the circumstances, but this was one of the worst cases Keith could remember.

'Good luck to the cleaning team,' he thought.

With his first plan, and the accompanying administration, completed, he checked his diary for the rest of the day. He had already briefly done so on arrival at work that morning, but it was always sensible to be 100% sure.

Two more plans to carry out in the morning: a GBH and a wounding—both to be done with Patrick. Then, and here was a first, a meeting in the afternoon with his line manager Barry Gallagher, one of the Deputy Governors of the prison, along with someone on a visit from the Home Office.

Might be interesting or boring. Difficult or easy, Keith thought. He had never been happy meeting those he thought of as 'The Knobs', but ten days ago Gallagher had "suggested" he and Patrick attend, and Keith had agreed. He couldn't really refuse. He knew very well that Gallagher wanted a couple of people who worked at 'the sharp end' to be present in order to handle specific questions relating to the actual operation of the new legislation.

Anyway, there was now a 15-minute break until the next plan needed to be implemented, so he walked over to the kettle to make himself a cup of coffee.

At this point, Patrick—who had been on holiday for the previous week—walked in.

"Good morning, Jerry Lee! How are you?!" Patrick Osobo thundered loudly.

Patrick was six foot four inches tall, and his personality sometimes made it appear as if he was simultaneously almost as wide. The tone of his deep voice suggested he was congratulating Keith on winning the lottery rather than simply giving him a standard greeting. Someone in the past had once described Patrick as 'clinically jolly', and Patrick, being Patrick, had readily embraced the shortened nickname 'CJ'.

Almost everyone at the prison had a nickname, and these were in common everyday usage. Among the staff, Gallagher's nickname was 'Wonderwall', although, needless to say, this was only used behind his back.

The official title of those responsible for ending the lives of those the court had condemned remained 'executioner'—but within the prison service, they were inevitably known as 'terminators' due to the manner of the court pronouncement that "your life will be terminated in accordance with the manner of death you inflicted on your victim".

The Senior Executioner (usually abbreviated to SE) at the prison was a jovial fifty-year-old named William Carruthers, whose passions in life—and almost his sole topics of conversation—were caravanning and rugby. He had accordingly, and perhaps unsurprisingly, been nicknamed 'Arnie'.

Keith, as his deputy, was known as 'Jerry Lee'. Not having much knowledge of the early days of rock and roll, Keith had to have it explained to him that this was because the legendary Jerry Lee Lewis from that era was known as 'The Killer'. Keith wasn't entirely happy with this, but knew that once a nickname was applied, it wasn't going to go away or change—so he accepted it. After a while, he had to concede it did seem to fit.

Keith liked Patrick, who—as he had—once served in the armed forces. Keith had joined the army at 18. Out of deference to his parents, he had stayed at school to do his A levels, which he neither enjoyed nor particularly excelled at. Three grade Ds. He didn't mind and had promptly applied to join the Parachute Regiment.

The selection was gruelling—way beyond what he expected it to be—but he never doubted he would succeed. Which he did. Ten years he had served. He had learned about violence, aggression, and the control of these. He had seen (what he would describe to non-veterans as) 'a lot' on his tours of duty abroad.

Patrick had been a lieutenant in the Kenyan Army. He was meticulous and thoroughly reliable. The sort of person you could trust completely; fiercely loyal to his companions and always there to watch a mate's back. Keith often thought Patrick would have been a definite asset to the Paras.

"What have you done so far on this fine day?" Patrick continued at the same volume, without allowing Keith any time to answer his original enquiry. He then added, in a tone that suggested this was the rather more important question, "And is there some coffee for me?"

"One plan completed, and now I'm getting ready for the others," replied Keith, pointing to the hard copies of the files on his desk.

Patrick glanced at them. "And in answer to your second question—yes, there is. I'll get you some."

He knew exactly how Patrick liked his coffee, so he made no further comment; he had no desire to hear the old joke, heard countless times, that Patrick wanted it *'black and mighty strong – just like me'*—which would be accompanied by a deep, raucous laugh that could go on for some time.

"Ah yes. Yes," said Patrick, still looking at the files on the desk. "Torville. I knew he was up for termination. All over the news. Him and his partner starved and beat up her 18-month-old kid."

Keith nodded.

"Didn't like it one bit, Jerry Lee. Didn't like it at all," Patrick continued. "They just gave that child salty water for ages, yeah? Post-mortem said the kid was all bashed up, wasn't he?"

Keith, who had just finished making the coffee, nodded again while holding out Patrick's drink.

Patrick accepted the cup. "You dealt with him OK?" he asked, looking Keith straight in the eye.

It was a valid question and could have meant one—or possibly both—of two things. One meaning was: *did you only do what you were supposed to do regardless of your feelings about the crime?* The other was: *are you still 'alright' with the process of going about killing someone in this way?*

"Strictly according to TAPP," replied Keith, assuming the question referred to the former. "As always. ETD tonight or tomorrow."

"Same happening to the mother?"

"I guess so. She's in Bronzefield. It'll be all over the media when it happens."

Patrick changed the subject. "So, we've got two to do until the big meeting later then? See, despite my holiday, I remembered it!" He added the last sentence in a mock proud tone.

Keith, who knew that Patrick was always fully prepared for a day's work and would have checked his own diary at home before he came in, just smiled.

"What's this meeting all about, Jerry Lee? Why do they want *us* there?"

"It's some guy from the Home Office. Governor is away, so Wonderwall wants to show how well all the new stuff is going and how brilliantly we're doing it. I suppose we just nod and agree with everything. Apparently"—he paused for dramatic effect—"we'll be getting real coffee, not instant."

"Hoo hoo, that'll make it worthwhile then!" roared Patrick, with one of his belly laughs that went on and on, interspersed with his repeating the words *'real coffee'*.

When it finally ended, he asked, "So before that, we've got the two plans?"

"Yup. Sholl—the GBH. And then Dudley—the wounding."

"Let me finish my coffee," said Patrick, "and then we'll go down there. You can do the admin afterwards," he said, then, noticing Keith's sharp glance, added, "My week off's made me forget what we have to do."

"Nice try, CJ," Keith replied.

"Worth a shot though, wasn't it?" Patrick chuckled loudly.

"No, it wasn't," replied Keith, who shook his head, pretending to despair.

***

Stuart Sholl was manacled to the wall opposite the cell door, with electronic metal grips around his ankles, knees, hips, chest, arms and head. Keith and Patrick walked in, having carefully checked the prisoner's identity against his cell location. Patrick closed the door. Sholl glanced briefly at them, then looked at the floor. He said nothing.

Keith carefully eyed both him and the way the manacles were holding him. He knew that hitting someone fixed rigidly to a wall with metal clamps wasn't as straightforward as it might seem; you didn't want to accidentally damage your hand or wrist.

Keith made a decision. He walked straight up to Sholl and hit him extremely hard in the stomach. Sholl gave a groaning sort of gasp, but that was choked off by Patrick's brutal karate chop to his throat.

Keith pressed a green button on the cell wall, and the clamps unlocked. Sholl fell forward. He didn't fall far, because Keith kicked him with all the force he could muster in the testicles, and as he doubled over, Keith followed the kick with a knee to Sholl's face, which shattered his nose.

With Sholl now tumbling backwards, Patrick moved in and punched him with a crushing blow to the right side of the head, and then one to the left. He then barely had to tap Sholl on the shoulders to cause him to fall face down onto the floor.

"Thirty seconds," said Keith, who had memorised the plan. For that duration, they both repeatedly kicked at the prone figure as if they were attempting to take a powerful penalty in a crucial game of football. Sholl, out of instinct, tried to protect his head insofar as he could after the blows he had already taken. He was never going to be very successful.

With the plan completed, Keith set the timer on the cell wall to electronically alert the medical team to attend the cell in fourteen minutes. It had taken fourteen minutes for an ambulance to be called to the scene where Sholl and another had meted out an identical assault on his victim.

"So," said Patrick as they closed the cell door and walked down the corridor. "Straight on to Dudley. I'll do all the admin. Quick lunch, then we can go to the meeting with old Wonderwall. Don't want to be late, eh?"

Keith nodded, agreeing on all counts.

Marcus Dudley was in a cell, manacled electronically in the same manner that Stuart Sholl had been. Unlike Sholl, he started to scream as soon as the door opened and he saw Keith and Patrick, both dressed in standard blood protection suits.

Keith and Patrick knew that they needed to start the plan as soon as possible. Even so, Keith asked Patrick a question.

"Just want to be sure. Did he cut the face or stab him first?"

"Stabbed him. The judge commented that the face cut was particularly something or other—gratuitous."

"That's what I thought. Right side. Wanted to be 100%," replied Keith, who picked up one of the designated knives from the trolley alongside Dudley, who had stopped screaming and had closed his eyes.

Without any hesitation, Keith stabbed him with a deep thrust in the middle of his ribcage on the left side of his body. Dudley screamed a cry that sounded like *"Waaaharraraaar."*

Patrick picked up one of the other knives with his right hand. He looked at it for a moment, then transferred it to his left hand. He seemed to weigh it temporarily, then suddenly swung it very quickly, cutting deeply into Dudley's right cheek, exposing the cheekbone and causing a torrent of blood to start pouring.

"End of," said Keith, pressing the green button to alert the medics to attend in twenty-two minutes' time, as per the plan. The two of them both moved towards the door, taking the trolley and knives with them.

"Release the clamps, CJ."

Patrick pressed another button, which released the manacles that had held Dudley to the wall. He slid, rather than fell, onto the floor. There was a lot of blood.

The last thing Dudley ever heard was a voice saying:

"...impressive... with your left hand... you're right-handed like me... I've never really been able to hold..."

***

Gallagher's room was quite large and expansive – as befitted his status, he told himself. He wondered if the Governor's holiday this week was in any way related to the visit of Iain Beattie from the Home Office, and the fact that someone else would therefore have to deal with him. He suspected that it was. He could handle it, of course – he knew that. As an ambitious man, he also knew that the further he progressed in the prison service, the more he would have to handle these sorts of events.

He was understandably wary of people like Beattie. He'd done some research, of course, and Beattie was a very junior minister, not long in post. Gallagher was still wary; even the great and the good had to start somewhere, and they usually had long memories of those who had helped or hindered them on their journey to the top. He'd have to be careful. So would Keith and Patrick, but he knew he had no need to tell them that. That was, after all, why he had chosen them.

He had wondered, briefly, whether he should ask Patrick – in a polite and jokey way, obviously – to 'tone it down a bit', just for once. On reflection, and it only took a second or two, he'd decided not to bother; he might as well ask the sun to stop shining.

In the event, he need not have worried.

Keith and Patrick were precisely on time for the meeting. Gallagher welcomed them in.

"This is Mr Beattie, the minister I told you about," he declared, rather overdoing the enthusiastic tone.

Keith and Patrick walked into the office and shook hands with Beattie.

"Let's all sit down," Gallagher went on, unnecessarily pointing to the chairs at a sizable oak table in the middle of the room. In front of each chair was a new notepad and pen, along with two bottles of water: one sparkling and one still.

"The minister and I have already had a chat about how the new policies are working, but Mr Beattie would like to hear from you."

Patrick shared Gallagher and Keith's opinion of people like Beattie and eyed him warily. Beattie launched into a short monologue as to how he was 'on a fact-finding mission' and was 'keen to learn from the experts'. Gallagher, Keith and Patrick had collectively chuckled politely and murmured their appreciation when he first used those words. Beattie, however, went on to repeat them three more times during the meeting, which rather diminished their impact and eventually served only to annoy.

"Is there anything we can do to improve things?" Beattie asked at one point. He added hastily, "Of course, we've only just started, but we are always open to suggestions from those in the know."

Keith and Patrick were wise to such flattery, but at least he hadn't said 'the experts' again. Like employees in any organisation, they were fully aware of the bureaucracy, the IT failures, the personality clashes, the 'office politics' and everything else that prevented that organisation from operating smoothly — but they were much too savvy to say anything.

Beattie looked expectantly at them. There was an embarrassing pause where no one said anything.

"Well, there is one thing," said Patrick, who noticed Gallagher immediately widen his eyes and adopt a 'be very careful' expression. "The recruitment could be better. It's done centrally now, isn't it? Some are no good. We lost two new ones recently. They didn't even last a week. The first one lasted four days. He walked out. And as for the other one…"

"The other one?" queried Beattie.

"He didn't follow instructions, sir," said Patrick. "He was on straightforward assault plans to start with, as everyone is, but he kept going way beyond what he was supposed to do. Beyond TAPP."

"I dismissed him for unprofessional conduct at the end of his second day," said Gallagher.

Beattie, who had ignored the notepad on the table and was tapping briskly on his tablet, said without looking up, "Quite right too. We can't have that. I'll pass it on."

He continued tapping away for a while.

"Now then," he continued, finally looking up, "I know you have that bomber to deal with later this afternoon. You're all prepared?"

"Our SE is on leave following a family bereavement, and so Keith will be in charge," said Gallagher.

"I see. Four-thirty, isn't it?"

"Four-thirty is when we set the timer, sir," said Keith.

"Of course. Of course," replied Beattie hastily.

"Would you like to be present with Keith and Patrick, Minister?" asked Gallagher, although he knew what the response was going to be.

"No, thank you. I've got to get back and make my report – on all the good work that's going on here."

Beattie added the latter comment after rather obviously having had a happy flash of inspiration.

"Of course, Minister," said Gallagher.

Beattie stood up, gathering his tablet and briefcase, just as the phone rang. Gallagher answered.

"Barry Gallagher," he said and listened for a moment. "Ah, Robert." There was a pause. "I see. Actually, Keith's here now. I could pass you over." Another pause. "Yes, sure."

He looked at Keith and said, "Mr Pleasance." He then looked at Beattie and said in an almost theatrical tone, "All will be revealed, Minister."

Once Keith knew who was on the end of the phone, he immediately guessed the likely reason for the call. Robert Pleasance, who had the simple title of *Senior Administrator*, which belied his many considerable responsibilities, was the only person in the prison Keith knew who didn't have a nickname – or if he did, no one ever used it.

"Good afternoon, Mr Pleasance. How can I help you?"

"I just wanted to speak about the job you did earlier. Dudley."

"Yes, sir. All done according to the plan."

"I wouldn't expect anything less from you and Patrick," replied Mr Pleasance.

"Sir, I think I can guess why you are calling Mr Gallagher."

Beattie, who could only hear half of the conversation, looked distinctly unhappy about this and seemed as if he were about to say something, but Gallagher gave him a respectful 'just a moment' look.

Keith listened for a further ten or so seconds.

"Yes, I see. I'll tell Patrick – he's here too. Mr Gallagher will probably call you later when the meeting with the Minister has finished." Gallagher nodded crisply. "OK, so that's DWMA. NOK and ML protocols commenced. Yes, sir. Thank you for letting me know."

Beattie couldn't contain himself any longer.

"Clearly something significant has occurred," he said stiffly. "Something I need to be aware of? And those acronyms...?"

"Would you care to translate for the Minister, Keith?" asked Gallagher.

"Well, sir, Dudley – who we dealt with this morning – stabbed someone in the ribs and slashed him across the face outside a country pub about seven months ago. So, he was sentenced accordingly. The person he stabbed survived, but only just. Due to the location of the pub and also because of a burst water main blocking the traffic, it took twenty-two minutes from the 999 call to the arrival of the ambulance."

Beattie still looked puzzled.

"Well sir, DWMA means 'Dead When Medics Arrived'. There must have been no pulse. As you know, there's no resuscitation attempt when that happens after this sort of sentence. NOK means 'Next of Kin'. Mr Pleasance's team will be informing them, probably right now, as to what happened and giving details of how to collect the body. ML is 'Media Liaison'. They will be releasing details in the usual way."

"That's certainly an aspect of the new regime that has operated well. Their statements are usually brief and factual," said Beattie.

Keith nodded. "I can only speak for this prison, sir, but Mr Pleasance— in fact, all the administration here — is very efficient."

Gallagher positively beamed at this. "You're sure you don't want to stay for TAPP of the bomber, Minister? If not, perhaps just a quick tour of the facilities before you go?"

Beattie, who had no desire to be on the premises during an execution, glanced at his watch. "Well, perhaps yes, a very quick tour if you can arrange one."

"Straight away. No problem. Keith and Patrick will look after you and bring you back here afterwards, or escort you back to the gate."

It had dawned on both Keith and Patrick that they would be the ones responsible for the tour as soon as Gallagher had mentioned it.

"Our pleasure, sir. Come with us," said Keith.

Gallagher made various comments to the Minister about how pleased he was to meet him which, although not exactly 'cringeworthy', nevertheless came pretty close.

Patrick led the way while recapping for Beattie what had happened in the case of Denny Seabrooke, the bomber.

The bombing of a West Country council meeting seven months previously, by a member of a tiny environmental group almost no one had ever heard of, had been a complete surprise. Two people had been killed — members of the public, not councillors. Seabrooke had tried to throw a bag containing a homemade bomb into the council chamber from the back of the public gallery, but it had fallen short and landed against the balcony, where it detonated ten seconds later, killing two people who had come to watch the meeting.

Why this had happened was never established, Patrick explained. At the previous council meeting, there was a suggestion of building a new housing estate because of increased availability of government funding, which would have entailed the destruction of some ancient woodland, but nothing had progressed beyond a very early series of tentative proposals.

Seabrooke had alluded, vaguely, to "killing the countryside" in his police interview, but afterwards simply shouted obscenities at everyone, including his own lawyer. It was not clear if he had intended to end his own life at the same time as he threw the bomb. In fact, a huge amount was unclear about the whole event, including how he knew how to make the bomb — or even if it was him who had made it.

After he eventually pleaded 'not guilty', the matter went to trial, where he went back to simply shouting obscenities. After less than ten minutes, he was removed to the cells. The same thing happened the next day — in fact, for the whole duration of the trial.

"Quite understandable. The Authorised Judicial Manager had no choice," commented Beattie.

Patrick, now near the end of the tale, remarked that there had been some suggestion — in fact, a strong suggestion from his lawyer right at the start — that Denny Seabrooke had not been mentally competent to plead in the first place.

Beattie was dismissive of this. "Amongst other things, the new guidelines revised and streamlined all that sort of thing to bring it up to date. For years it seemed as if almost every defence advocate claimed their client had some sort of mental issue. Every lunatic religious fanatic, every violent thug, and every crazed environmental protester apparently wasn't responsible for what they'd done. The law-abiding and hardworking public were fed up with it."

"Well, we just do our job, sir, after the court has decided," said Patrick noncommittally.

"Oh, look out!"

The corridor they had just turned into was strewn with wires, ladders, dust sheets and various tools. Work was obviously in progress in the room to their right, about five metres ahead. Intense hammering and swearing suggested it currently wasn't going well.

They stopped briefly at the opening to the room. No door was in place yet. They could see what looked like a sort of metal bed, and next to it, a kind of mechanical arm — similar to, but much more substantial than, the sort with a light on it that a dentist would use to shine into someone's mouth.

"This bloody shit never works!" shouted one of the workmen in the room, angrily throwing some sort of electrical device onto the floor, not noticing those who were peering in from the corridor.

"That's going to be the rape suite," said Keith. "Not finished yet," he added, rather unnecessarily. "Anyway, this way, sir."

The Explosive Execution Cell (EEC) was one of only two in England. It was for the use of those who had killed others by the use of a bomb. It was a small room, two and a half metres wide and just under three metres long, with walls lined with thick steel plate. There was a similarly solid metal chair attached to the back wall with metal clamps for arms, wrists, waist, knees, ankles and head. Like those in other cells, these were electronically operated and 'clicked into place', rather than being old-fashioned leather ones that needed to be tied. They were also easier to clean.

Prisoners who were due to die were told that they could either 'go quietly' and sit in the chair, whereupon the clamps would be activated, or, if they became awkward, they would be tasered into submission and clamped in anyway. It was made perfectly clear that they would end up in the chair one way or the other.

There had only been four people executed in this way since the law was changed, and the attitude of the prisoners was currently 3-1 in favour of 'going quietly'. Keith reported this to Beattie.

One metre away from the chair was another solid piece of metal — a slab of it, 150 cm high, attached very securely into the floor. This had fixtures facing the chair that enabled the explosive charge to be attached to it. The whole floor of the cell resembled a cattle grid.

How long the device took to explode was randomly generated by a computer once the device was armed — anywhere between three minutes and a maximum of two hours. This was in accordance with the principle of letting the punishment fit the crime. The people (or person) who had been killed by the bomber hadn't known when in their life they were going to die. The prisoners obviously did know they were going to die — but didn't know exactly when. Parliament had decided this was acceptable.

Following the detonation, an area of the 'cattle grid' just in front of the chair would swing open, the electronic clamps around the deceased would unlock, the chair would tilt forwards, and whatever solid material was left would slide into a standard army body bag positioned beneath that part of the cell. This was then removed to a temporary storage area nearby.

Barely noticeable on the walls of the EEC were some metal protrusions that looked vaguely like eggs. These were actually part of a sprinkler system designed not to be affected by the blast. They were switched on after the remains of the executed had gone into the body bag and been removed. These sprayed the room with water imbued with a variety of sterilising chemicals.

After about ten minutes, the Residual Cleaning Team entered the cell fully 'suited up', toting high-pressure hoses to remove anything that remained. Under the floor was a mesh filter that caught any lingering parts of bone or flesh. These were then emptied into the nearby body bag, which subsequently went to the morgue. The water and blood flowed away into some sort of tank. Keith had occasionally wondered whether this was then simply released into the prison's sewage system like any other waste. No one seemed to know.

Beattie said nothing while walking to the EEC, listening to Keith and Patrick's explanation of how it operated.

Keith assumed that Beattie knew that death by execution—like any death—had to be duly certified by a doctor, but he mentioned it anyway. Doctor Amanda Harris was the medical professional attached to the prison responsible for this. She had the well-deserved nickname of 'Hardarse'. A sixty-three-year-old retired GP, she was brusque to the point of offending almost everyone she came into contact with. Most people tried to avoid her.

Hardarse Harris had made it quite clear from the moment she was appointed that, post-detonation, she would 'take a look from the doorway of the cell' and that this look would be sufficient for her to sign the necessary documentation. She had told the prison governor bluntly that she knew exactly what an explosive detonation at very close range in a confined area would do to a human and that she had no intention of—what she described as—'rooting around in the slop trying to find something to take a pulse from'. The governor had not argued.

Her office was on the way to the EEC and, as it turned out, she was already present, the door open, tapping away on her laptop.

They stopped outside. Harris looked up sharply, as if to say, *What are you people doing here?* Keith picked up on this at once and explained to Beattie who she was.

"Nice to meet you, Doctor," Beattie said enthusiastically. "Always good to see someone committed to the new regime."

"I'm just doing a job," Harris replied bluntly. "And as for the new regime—you must have been concerned when half the judiciary resigned when you brought it in."

"Forty-two point three percent, actually," replied Beattie smoothly, albeit clearly annoyed at the nature of the comment.

"Didn't hundreds more take early retirement?" Harris returned acidly. "A large number of prison service staff left too, as I recall."

As if following a prepared script, Beattie continued, "Those who left for whatever reason were quickly replaced. In the courts, for example, a very large number of people were very happy to put themselves forward for the newly created post of Authorised Judicial Manager, which replaced the role of judge and magistrate. With someone who has the proper judicial authority to manage the court and deal with the sentence, we can do without those who feel unable to carry out their duties as demanded by the will of Parliament. We're also rather proud of the NSA—the New Sentencing Algorithm."

"I know what NSA stands for. I'm not stupid," snapped Harris, turning her eyes back to her screen.

They all knew what it stood for. Previously, when someone was found or pleaded guilty, judges and magistrates had followed a set of sentencing guidelines to arrive at a verdict. The guidelines did not produce a single immutable outcome; they gave a range of sentencing options, so there was always an element of 'what should I/we do given these particular circumstances?' in the decision. This had now ceased. The aggravating and mitigating factors were entered into a computer containing the appropriate software, and the algorithm produced the definitive sentence—which The Authorised Judicial Manager then announced.

Beattie, clearly unaccustomed to being spoken to in such a manner, felt the need to assert himself. "The new 'Right First Time' codes of practice for prosecution and defence—and the penalties for not adhering to them—do rather seem to have concentrated minds. And the abolition of frivolous appeals has sped up the whole process of justice," he went on.

"Justice? Really? Glad you think so," said Harris, tapping on her keyboard without looking up.

"I've heard enough," he said, referring as much to Harris as to the EEC and its operation. "If you two could kindly take me back to the gate, my driver should be around somewhere. Thank Mr Grosvenor—sorry, Mr Gallagher," he said, slightly flustered, "for all his cooperation. *He*"—the word was emphasised—"couldn't have been more helpful."

"Of course, sir," replied Keith.

They walked down various corridors in silence, which Beattie, unable to contain himself any longer, eventually broke in a manner neither Keith nor Patrick was expecting.

"Jesus. She was a GP? I'm glad I was never treated by her," he said venomously. "A starving fucking vampire in the middle of the night would have a better bedside manner."

Patrick tried to stifle a giggle at this and managed to turn it into a cough. Keith glanced sharply at him, albeit with some slight amusement showing on his own face.

"I couldn't comment, sir," he said formally. Patrick 'coughed' again.

They escorted Beattie back to the prison entrance and, with the appropriate comment along the lines of "thank you for taking the time to come down here when you are obviously busy," left him there.

Gallagher was delighted to hear about this comment later in the day and made a mental note to do both Keith and Patrick a favour sometime in the future. He was less happy on learning about Hardarse's behaviour, but Harris was not actually an employee of the prison service, so he decided to let the governor deal with her—if he chose to—on his return.

"Well, that's it for the day, CJ," said Keith. "I think we did well on all counts."

"Certainly did, Jerry Lee. But you know..." replied Patrick, who then paused.

"What is it?" asked Keith. "Something on your mind?"

"I've got to say, I'm never happy when people like that come around looking at me."

Keith nodded. "At least he didn't ask a stupid question like 'do you enjoy your work?' And Wonderwall seemed pleased. He owes us."

"Yeah, but you know what we were at that meeting, Jerry Lee? Just boxes. Boxes to tick. To tick to say he's spoken to people like us."

"You're not wrong," replied Keith. "But it's just the way things are."

"I know, I know. I just—I don't like it," Patrick sighed. "But you know the worst thing, the absolute worst thing about all of this stuff today is, Jerry Lee?"

Keith pouted and shrugged in a *no, so tell me* manner.

"We never got that real coffee," said Patrick in a deadpan voice.

His subsequent laughter was even louder and went on for even longer than usual.

Reflection

Is the behaviour of the characters credible?

A Different Approach

Sally Fraser sat down on—although 'collapsed onto' would have been a more appropriate term—her sofa. She felt dizzy and not a little sick.

"What have I done?" she asked out loud. She then repeated the question, again out loud, this time with emphasis on the word *'have'*.

She stared numbly at her TV screen. It was the 7.00 am BBC regional news. One topic dominated it: the bizarre and violent incidents in the town yesterday evening.

She told herself she could be going crazy thinking what she was thinking, but deep down—in fact, not deep down at all; very near the surface—she knew she wasn't. Too many dots joined up. She was sure she was responsible for what had happened.

Oh, it would never be blamed on her. After all, it wasn't *her* who had committed the crimes. It wasn't *her* who had suggested the crimes. No one would ever link her with the crimes.

If she had been thinking rationally, she might have realised that she was being rather too hard on herself. But she wasn't thinking rationally. Unsurprisingly.

She didn't think the situation was going to improve either. On the contrary, things were likely to get worse. Very much worse. Even if they *did* improve, she'd have to live with what she'd done and its consequences forever. That was going to be something that would be very difficult to do.

Sally worked for the town council at a senior level. She was one of those who led the negotiations over the contracts for the council's outsourced services. When preliminary negotiations had taken place with suppliers, these contracts were then always scrutinised by at least one council committee. When a contract passed that stage, it finally went to the councillors for approval.

On this journey, there were many problems that could—and did—arise. Draft contracts often went back and forth between the relevant committee and the service provider several times.

It was often left for Sally to 'smooth out any last-minute wrinkles' (as her line manager liked to say) one-on-one with the service provider before the contract came back to the committee for final approval and then went to the council for the formal vote. Sally was very good at smoothing out last-minute wrinkles.

It had been just over two months ago when she had the 'smoothing out wrinkles' meeting with Mr Dominic Bannister, CEO of DBZT Ltd. At the time, it had looked to Sally to be a very straightforward session. Indeed, it had been.

The matter in hand was to employ a private firm, DBZT Ltd, to issue fixed penalty fines to individuals under the council's new approach to littering. The previous provider of this service had gone into liquidation several months previously and had been highly ineffective. The contract would have been terminated anyway if the firm's financial problems had not sealed its fate first.

Councillors were fed up (and worried about losing their seats) with receiving comments that were essentially variations on remarks such as: "This place [insert road or specific location] is an absolute tip." "I bet you don't have to live with this sort of mess around your house." "Your inaction on clearing it up just encourages others to treat it as a dumping ground." "What am I paying my council tax for?" and "Why don't you do something about the problem?"

The comments were often phrased considerably more forcefully than this.

The police, naturally, had rather more important matters to deal with than litter, and the problem had been getting worse. The contract had gone out to tender, and it looked as though DBZT would be awarded it—subject to wrinkle-smoothing.

"This is a key initiative that we must get right," Sally had said. "The committee and I have read your submission. Your quote is in line with our budget, and we like what you've told us about the company. It certainly meets the expectations of a provider for this sort of service."

Mr Bannister nodded in a 'that's good' manner.

"The advantage of my company's operation is that I don't need to employ a small army out there 24/7 at great expense to you," he replied. "We just need the right people, at the right time, in the right place. And that will happen. My people are flexible and very dedicated. You tell me where the hotspots are—for, say, fly-tipping, or just ordinary littering—and we'll regularly visit them and deal with those causing the problem.

"But there will also"—he put emphasis on this word—"be roving patrols all over the town in places like car parks and play areas. These should be very effective. Word will get around. It will get around that whoever you are, this sort of action has consequences. The 'ZT' in DBZT stands for 'zero tolerance'."

He paused for a moment and then added, in a manner that suggested he was taking Sally into his confidence, "I'll be honest with you; I really want this to succeed. I'd like to use this as a flagship contract to publicise my company. I've got extensive plans for its growth."

It was Sally's turn to nod.

"Things must be done correctly though. Some people—and possibly, well probably, the media—are going to criticise this new approach as petty and over the top. It isn't, of course. The council needs to show it means business while acting in the proper manner."

"I understand what you're saying," replied Mr Bannister reassuringly. "Don't worry; my people may be a bit unusual, but they aren't like some sixteen-stone nightclub bouncer who's looking for trouble!" He chuckled in a way that invited Sally to join in.

"No, no. They understand the powers that they have and will use them to get the job done. We have a different approach. In fact, that's our mission statement."

Sally flipped idly through the contract she was holding. She had read it several times.

"This seems fine. However, naturally, I need to raise the issue of—and unambiguously clarify—exactly what happens if your service provision turns out not to be acceptable. Being blunt, the circumstances under which the contract will be terminated."

"You won't terminate the contract," said Mr Bannister very quickly. He smiled encouragingly. "Neither will I."

The meeting went on for almost another hour and a half. Sally didn't like wrinkles, which was why she was so good at her job. By the end of the meeting, there were none left.

At least not legally speaking. There was something about Mr Bannister and his way of speaking. Sally couldn't pin it down, couldn't articulate the slight concern in her head at all—but throughout almost the whole of the meeting, that 'something' had been at the back of her mind.

His choice of words had, on several occasions, seemed slightly odd to her, as if there was another meaning behind them. It wasn't an attempt by Mr Bannister to make the contract in some way equivocal and biased in his company's favour—she'd have spotted and ended that immediately. It was just something odd.

Well, she had reflected to herself while they had a break for a cup of coffee, *we all have our little quirks*. Twenty minutes after that, with the legal issues completed, she had said she could recommend its acceptance to the committee and could see no reason why the council itself was likely to reject it.

Mr Bannister was clearly very pleased, and he spoke with considerable enthusiasm.

"Once we get the formal go-ahead, DBZT will start as it means to go on. You'll notice a difference very quickly. Like I said earlier, word will get around about what is happening."

Apart from a few bits of small talk on the way down to the car park, that was it. They shook hands, and Mr Bannister drove away.

The committee duly approved the awarding of the contract, and three days later the council voted almost unanimously to accept it. As stated in that contract, DBZT Ltd started its work across the town exactly a month later.

It was four days after the contract became operational that Sally collapsed onto her sofa, looking aghast at the local news on her television.

***

It wasn't what she'd usually do at all. Nina Hallum was a 'Green' person and a Green voter—dutiful in her recycling and composting duties.

Nina had been on a diet for over two months. She'd stuck religiously to her reduced-calorie intake instructions, as well as doing the suggested accompanying exercises. It had worked. She'd lost weight and was feeling pleased with herself.

Weighing herself that morning, she had hardly believed the scales—but they were correct.

Then, on arriving at work, she had been summoned to see her line manager, Julie, *immediately*. All sorts of things flashed through her mind, but it turned out that Julie—who could never resist a bit of drama—after asking, "Do you know why I've called you in here?" (Nina didn't answer and simply shook her head), told Nina that her latest appraisal had been very positive and that an immediate pay rise to the next point on the pay spine was currently being processed.

Nina was delighted and spent most of the morning basking in a glow of achievement. The pay rise was no more than she deserved, of course (she told herself), but it was nice to see her achievements recognised. And achievements meant rewards.

So, at lunchtime, in addition to her low-calorie sandwich, she bought a choc ice to treat herself and ate it in the sunshine in the

Community Garden, which was situated just down the road from her workplace.

The ice cream provided a rush of sweetness; by God, it was good. So good, in fact, that when she'd finished eating it, perhaps her aim with the wrapper was affected—and when she threw it towards the bin, it missed and hit the ground.

She knew she should pick it up, but with the sun being so hot, the wrapper had become really sticky because the bar had started to melt, and she'd already got some chocolate over her hand. She used up several tissues trying to clean her fingers.

She stood up and dropped the tissues in the bin. She had been about to use another tissue to pick up the sticky wrapper to drop it in the bin when she noticed a stranger walking towards her.

She knew many people from the other firms nearby who used the garden, but not this man. She felt slightly nervous for some reason. She thought he said, "Excuse me, but..." But nothing—Nina was not going to speak to a man she didn't know, who made her feel uneasy, especially as she could see he was the only other person in the garden. There was no CCTV. You never knew what might happen, even in broad daylight, she told herself.

She ignored him, left the wrapper on the ground, and walked quickly towards the garden's gate. She felt perfectly secure once she was through it and onto the crowded pavement. She took a quick glance over her shoulder back towards the garden, but the man was nowhere to be seen.

***

Andy Rafferty, by contrast, didn't give the proverbial 'monkeys' about litter. He had won £5,000 on a scratch card just over a month ago. This had temporarily ended his very unenthusiastic attempts to find work.

Now, while the weather was warm, his day invariably followed the exact same routine. He got up about 10:30, had a cup of tea, watched some TV, and set off for the park. He liked to spend as much time as possible away from the single room that he lived in, which was part of a (very) multiple occupancy house.

On the way to the park, he would stop at the small parade of shops next to it. He'd go into the newsagent for a paper and a packet of cigarettes, walk two shops down to buy four or five cans of super-strength lager or cider at 'Bargain Booze', and then nip next door into 'Sammy's Chicken Shop', where he'd buy a bucket of greasy fried chicken and chips.

Armed with all of this, he'd walk into the park and settle down to eat, read, drink and smoke on one of the benches on the south side of its lake. The bench had a nice view of the ducks and other birds that waddled around during the day, hoping to be fed. Andy liked the birds. They didn't judge him.

Andy had become something of a fixture in the park since winning the money. Despite his rather dishevelled appearance, he was never threatening, never begged for money, and never caused any trouble—unless you counted his regular disappearances into the undergrowth by the side of the pond to relieve his bladder. This obvious reason for his disappearances understandably tended to upset those who saw it, especially those with young children, as he tended to both enter and exit the bushes fiddling with the front of his trousers.

Also, not everyone appreciated his cheery wave and slightly— or very—slurred (depending on how long he had been sitting there), "Howya doing?" as they walked past.

However, bush visits and indistinct greetings aside, it was the growing pile of discarded cans, food scraps and cigarette butts that really was unwelcome—particularly as the park didn't have the funds to pay someone to empty its bins or pick up litter every day. It was unsightly, and the discarded food encouraged rats.

With the alcohol, once he'd finished one can, Andy would lob it half-heartedly to his left, where there was a bin. Sometimes the can landed in the bin (at which Andy would smile and think, "Two points!" recalling the days long, long ago when he'd played basketball), but most of the time it didn't. Then he'd start on the next one. The same attempt at a lob went for the remains of the chicken meal, the wrappers it came in, and his cigarette ends.

On the day that was to change his life forever, things were no different. He'd been in the park since about half past one, and when he got up to leave it was nearly four.

On that day, either the strength of the alcohol was even more 'super' than usual, or the bright sun had affected him—or both. When Andy stood up to walk home, he felt very unsteady on his feet, much more so than usual. His head throbbed almost painfully; this wasn't the usual nicely 'muzzy' feeling he usually got.

But he had a solution for this sort of situation, which he had used before.

"Gotta soak up the booze, soon as," he muttered to himself. He thought he might call in for some more chicken on the way home, but then he remembered that Sammy's didn't reopen until five o'clock. No problem, he reflected, recalling that he had some of Sammy's finest in the fridge at home, left from a few days ago. Actually, he wondered, was it longer ago than that? Maybe even last week?

It didn't matter; he had something somewhere.

He wobbled into the bushes for one last visit. When he emerged, he immediately had the feeling that someone was watching him. It was a very odd sensation. He was right.

A short distance away, he could see that a man was not only looking straight at him but was apparently taking a picture of him with his phone.

"Wha' you wan'?" Andy half spoke, half belched.

The man said something that Andy didn't hear very clearly. He stared at the man for a moment, then turned away and started walking—at the same time waving his hand in a gesture that was a cross between a dismissive 'Whatever, I don't care' and the standard two-fingered salute.

***

Toby Pickering had recently retired from his job as a school caretaker and now devoted his life to the two things that mattered most to him: his two Husky dogs and fixing electric guitars. He did the latter very well indeed, and for quite nominal sums of money. He was happy just to be known as 'the guy who could always fix it' (whatever 'it' was), rather than charging the prices a music shop would.

Toby's house was semi-detached. Mr and Mrs Tormey's house was joined to the right side of his. Mr and Mrs Tormey, who were in their mid-70s, had been concerned at first, when he moved in, that his dogs would make a noise, but were delighted when they discovered how good-natured and well-behaved they were. Similarly, all fears about 'testing his guitars at high volume' proved groundless. They all got on very well. People liked Toby. They also liked his dogs.

Jimbo and Jambo were certainly very friendly dogs. Perfect pets, some might say. Even someone who was not normally 'a dog person' might well have agreed with that. They never leapt up at anyone who showed an interest in them, never tried to lick anyone, and never dribbled over them. They rarely even barked enthusiastically. They just wagged their tails exuberantly, happy to be the centre of attention. Which naturally encouraged the person patting them to do so even more, resulting in even faster tail wagging. Happy times all round.

The only thing about Toby and his dogs that was very regrettable was that he had never, ever, bothered with the 'picking up your dog shit craze' (as he put it). His dogs could 'go' where they wanted to, as far as he was concerned, and he wasn't going to bag it up afterwards. He didn't know anyone who had ever been fined for allowing a dog to foul a pavement or a grass verge—or, in fact, foul anywhere—and he doubted he ever would.

He did try to steer them clear of children's playgrounds and sports fields, but if the dogs did use these as a toilet, then so be it.

On the evening in question, during their final walk of the day, both dogs 'used' the road about 300 metres from his house. A woman was clearly watching both him and the dogs from her garden with open disapproval from across the street, but he was used to this sort of 'look' and studiously ignored her. She might have called out something, but Toby wasn't certain, and thought that even if she had, it wasn't necessarily directed at him.

Insofar as he gave it another thought, it was that if the forecast was correct, heavy rain was expected later—and so it would all be washed away anyway.

***

Sally's town, like most towns, had a pub called *The New Inn*. This one was next to a path that ran along the side of the river. If you walked out of the pub, turned left along the path and kept walking for a few hundred metres, there—almost right under *The Old Iron Bridge*—was a large wooden bench. Carved into the bench, in fading lettering, was: *In loving memory of Emily Washington*.

Sadly, for the friends and/or relatives of Emily Washington, no one who walked along that path now had any memory of her at all—loving or otherwise. She might have been a local councillor who selflessly devoted her life to working for those in the area, or she might have been someone who just liked walking her dog along that section of the path. Or neither.

Nathan and 'AJ', two drug dealers, simply referred to this loving memorial to Emily Washington as *The Bench*, as did their clients. This was where they 'worked' from.

It was an ideal spot. They could see anyone approaching for over a hundred metres in each direction; they were right next to the bridge if it rained; and there was *The New Inn* just around the bend of the path to their right—a couple of minutes' walk away—if they wanted a drink. The river, while not particularly wide or fast-flowing, could be used to dispose of 'material' if required. The current would still carry away anything they threw into it fairly quickly, making 'proof of ownership' difficult.

This disposal of material had not been necessary recently; the police seemed to have lost interest in them, or perhaps currently had other priorities. Nowadays, Nathan and AJ simply used the river for the disposal of their cigarettes.

That afternoon, around quarter past five, they concluded several deals with some regular customers. Then there was a lull in calls to them. Nothing new there. Business would pick up later. It always did as the day wore on.

Not being great conversationalists, they sat listening to some music from Nathan's phone while chain smoking. They both always smoked down to the filter and then had a contest to see who could flick the butt furthest into the river. There was no need to count 'one, two, three...' to start this contest; they just looked at each other and flicked.

On this occasion, AJ's didn't even reach the water. Nathan laughed in a 'what was that?!' manner.

Suddenly, there was a voice from behind their bench.

"Are you going to pick that up?"

AJ and Nathan were used to situations when people got mouthy. They were both ready to use violence without a second thought when challenged, and so they weren't particularly concerned when they heard the voice. This was especially true when they turned around and saw that the man who had spoken was only about five foot nine inches tall, with a very slight build.

But they were nevertheless rather surprised. Where had he come from? There had been no one on the path in either direction for nearly a quarter of an hour. That meant he must have come across the field behind them. But there was a barbed wire fence at the edge of that field, a few metres behind *The Bench*, and surely they'd have heard him approaching and climbing over it?

"It pollutes the river. Oh, and the birds and other animals try to eat it, which makes them ill," said the man in a matter-of-fact tone. "Please pick it up. If you don't, I'll have to start proceedings against you."

AJ and Nathan literally couldn't believe what they were hearing. Nathan wondered, albeit briefly, if this was some sort of wind-up organised by one of his friends. But as usual, he didn't think about any situation for long.

"Just fuck off, mate, before you get hurt," he said, while briefly opening his coat to show the handle of what was clearly a large kitchen knife.

"That's just what I was about to say to you," replied the stranger mildly. "Take all your rubbish—all of your rubbish, not just that cigarette end—with you. And don't come back making a mess and littering here. Ever. Otherwise, as I've already stated, there will be proceedings... and consequences."

Nathan and AJ exchanged a glance which communicated far more in a millisecond than any words they'd ever used, or were ever likely to use. It said: *Who is this fool?* (or something rather stronger). *He's obviously not the police. Doesn't he realise the implications of behaving like this on our territory? We can't tolerate being spoken to in this disrespectful manner. He's had fair warning already. Therefore, he needs to be taught a lesson he won't forget.*

They both stood up simultaneously, intent on delivering that lesson.

The man's body language didn't change at all. He didn't move to adopt an aggressive or even a defensive posture.

***

Sally sat on her sofa, unable to move. Yesterday's events in the town were being spelled out in ghastly and barely believable detail by the reporters.

The first incident that the police had been called to had occurred just before six o'clock. Persistent, loud, high-pitched screams from somewhere along the river had been heard from the beer garden of *The New Inn*. These went on and on for so long that the police were called.

Two men, well known to the police, had been found by the Old Iron Bridge. Each had his hands crossed one on top of the other. One of the men's crossed hands was on top of the other's, so that there was 'a stack of four'. A ten-inch kitchen knife had been driven right through this pile of hands and then nearly two inches into the arm of the wooden bench that all four hands were stacked upon. Both men had lost a lot of blood and were now in hospital. Initial suspicions were that it was gang-related, involving rival drug dealers.

Then there was the bizarre suicide of a Miss Nina Hallum at her home. She appeared to have forced sweet wrappers and other pieces of paper down her own throat until she was barely able to breathe. She had then thrown herself out of an upstairs window.

The report said that, at about seven o'clock, a couple out jogging had passed her house and seen her staggering around in a room upstairs, apparently drunk. She seemed to be 'coughing up pieces of paper', then 'sort of waved' (as one of them put it), before, to their horror, throwing herself against a partially open window and crashing heavily onto her front lawn.

The garden was full of litter – as was the one downstairs room of her house that was visible from the pavement. It was almost as if she had been storing up bags of rubbish for months and finally decided to tip them all over her previously immaculate front garden before... going on to do what she did.

When the Tormeys heard Jimbo and Jambo howling and barking continuously, they knew something must be wrong and were genuinely worried for their neighbour when this went on for nearly half an hour. They knew dogs often became distressed if something had happened to their owner. They left it another half an hour and then called the police—not 999; the non-emergency number.

The police had been having a busy evening, and so a visit to the Tormeys to try and discover the reason for continuous barking was never going to merit an urgent response. The Tormeys, after some considerable discussion, decided at about nine-thirty to investigate for themselves.

In the interview with the reporter later, Mrs Tormey said that "she wished to God they hadn't".

Toby didn't answer their knocks on his front door, but the dogs could be heard—obviously very agitated—barking behind it. The side gate to his back garden was open, and the two of them went into the garden and approached Toby's large shed, the door of which was slightly ajar.

On opening the door, they were confronted by what Mr Tormey (who was very visibly distressed in the interview) described as 'a scene from hell'.

He said, "The dogs weren't in the shed. They were in the house. But the whole place was knee-deep in dog... mess." (He'd rather obviously wanted to use a different word but couldn't bring himself to do so.) "I mean *knee-deep*. The smell. I'll never forget it. Toby was floundering around in it, on his stomach, almost totally covered and virtually choking on it. His dogs couldn't have done it. I mean, I spoke to him only yesterday in that very same shed and it was clean as a whistle. It was like all the dog mess in the whole town had been collected and dumped in there with him while he was..."

He turned away, unable to continue. The reporter quickly stepped in, and a link was made to the next incident.

This involved a Mr Andrew Rafferty.

The reporter said that Mr Rafferty was known to his neighbours as 'an eccentric character', but when he appeared in the street staggering around choking, vomiting blood, and eventually collapsing into the road—where he lay unmoving, which had stopped the traffic in both directions—it had obviously gone way beyond eccentricity and an ambulance had been called.

The person who had first approached him after he fell onto the road said that in his hand, he had a bag which had split open, spilling the remnants of what looked and smelled like putrid meat and mould-covered bones.

"Why would he be holding *that*?" he had asked.

***

Sally had taken in the details the reporters were giving and felt dizzy—and not a little sick—but suddenly her focus changed, and she was unable to think about anything except some of Mr Bannister's words, which now echoed in her head very clearly.

"DBZT will start as it means to go on. You'll notice a difference very quickly."

He had smiled as he said those words.

She now understood the meaning behind the phrases *"my people may be a bit unusual"* and *"they understand the powers they have and will use them to get the job done."*

She also recalled the comment: *"You won't terminate the contract."*

It hadn't been an *'oh don't worry about that side of things!'* sort of comment.

It had been a blunt statement of fact.

With her mind spinning, she was vaguely aware that the TV was now reporting more *breaking local news*, where a dead body had been found in an old freezer in a parking area well known for dumping and fly-tipping.

But by now, Sally couldn't watch any more.

Reflection

Did you expect the story to end in the way that it did?

Was what happened to Toby, Nathan, AJ, Nina and Andy their own fault?

The Very Terrible Thing

I suppose the worst aspect about anything that really scares any of us is that we never truly know why it scares us. OK, perhaps I'm wrong—maybe a psychiatrist or someone like that could try and explain it. But with The Very Terrible Thing, the problem was I never knew what it was and therefore never got close to knowing why it was so terrible.

From a very early age, I didn't like to visit Beckenham High Street. Not one bit. It wasn't the High Street itself that frightened me but what I experienced before I got to it. By that, I mean when we went shopping, Mum or Dad would park in a car park which was conveniently situated nearby. We'd leave the car park, turn left, and within a hundred metres there was a T-junction, and at the top of the 'T', running east to west (or vice versa), was the High Street.

Once we were there on the High Street, right in front of the T-junction, was a toy shop. 'Beckenham Toys' it was (unsurprisingly) called. It had—and this seems decidedly odd today—a little slot in the wall outside, and if you put a penny (an old penny—ever seen one?) in that slot, it made a toy train run round a track in the window for about a minute. This was amazing for a young child in the 1960s. I often put a penny in.

The problem was getting to that happy situation.

You see, as you came out of the car park and turned left, there was a church. A big church. Saint Someone-or-other. I suppose I could look it up online now, but what difference would it make? I can't be bothered. What most certainly did bother and frighten me badly back then was The Very Terrible Thing that was on the top of that church.

From a very early age I sensed—no, I knew—that something *bad* (that was the only word I could think of when I was about six) was up there, looking at me as I passed by. Then, as I got a bit older, I progressed to thinking of the thing as *terrible*. Now I suppose I'd use words like *malignant* or *evil*.

That feeling was so bad that I only ever dared look up at it once to try to see exactly what it was. That took a huge feat of courage for me. There was a shape up there; a human shape with a black cape and wearing what I suppose we'd call a hoodie now. I couldn't see any facial features—well, it was high up above the pavement and I could barely stand to look anyway. It was pointing down towards me.

Other than that, the nearest I can describe it—although I didn't know it at the time—is to say it looked vaguely like that Old Father Time thing on top of Lord's Cricket Ground. I don't follow cricket, and I've only seen that... whatever it is (weathervane?) a couple of times. You know when rain stops play and, scratching around for things to view other than highlights, a camera gets flashed onto it and the commentators say something about it. The Very Terrible Thing looked vaguely like it, but certainly wasn't *a quaint piece of history* or whatever the words are that they might use.

What was a bit odd was that although The Very Terrible Thing upset me—and terrified me—when I walked past the church, it never troubled me when I wasn't passing by. I never woke up in the night thinking about it (I think it was werewolves that were bothering me back then). It was always *only* when passing by that church on the way to the High Street.

Unfortunately, as we seemed to do a lot of shopping in the High Street, and I was too young to be left on my own at home when Mum and Dad shopped, I encountered it many times.

I remember on one occasion, when I suppose I must have been about seven, I went to the High Street with my father. We weren't food shopping; we went to buy a new vacuum cleaner at some electrical store. I didn't want to go because I knew The Very Terrible Thing would be up there on the church, but I put on the proverbial *brave face*.

We walked out of the car park and, although I tried to be strong, it didn't work. We turned left, and I froze. Stopped dead. It was up there, looking down.

At me.

As I knew it would be.

Dad must have said something like his usual good-natured "Come on, mate," but I didn't dare move. In fact, I couldn't. I decided I'd have to say something. Here's a good phrase: *I plucked up courage* and, having done so, pointed up towards the top of the church. Pointed. I dared not actually look. It was up there, and looking right at me.

"What's that up there?" I asked.

Dad looked up towards where I was pointing.

The Very Terrible Thing obviously wasn't visible to him. He latched onto something very different.

"That's called a steeple. The tower, the top of a church. A steeple. Or is it a spire? No, it's a steeple. Or is it? Steeple? Spire?" he muttered a couple of times, seemingly unsure.

I didn't care what the top of a church was called and replied, "No, not that bit. That other thing."

He looked up again. He still seemed puzzled as to what I was getting at, but then must have thought he knew what I was asking about.

"Oh that. It's a metal strip—a lightning rod, I think it's called. If there's a storm and there's lightning, then it hits the metal, not the steeple. It runs all the way down. See?" He pointed, tracing it down the side of the church. "It goes all the way to the pavement. If lightning hits the steeple, it could knock it down, but not if it hits the rod. It's a safety thing."

Well, I learned some stuff right there on that visit to the High Street, but it was no compensation for my fear. I've already said I didn't care about the correct word for the top of a church and, similarly, I didn't care about lightning rods either. Dad obviously couldn't see or sense what I could. Why?

Well, I got through that particular visit to the High Street, but there were many others like it that caused me similar levels of distress.

This all went on until I was about ten or eleven, I suppose. As I got older, I was deemed old enough to be left on my own at home instead of being dragged out 'to help with the shopping'. Then there came a time—I guess I was about thirteen—when one day I went to the High Street and The Very Terrible Thing just wasn't there anymore. I just saw a stone cross at the top of the church. That's what everyone else must have seen. It had gone.

Thinking back after all this time, when I was young, you know, I never asked myself, *Why doesn't The Very Terrible Thing like me?*

I do wonder now.

Over the years, whenever I've thought about The Very Terrible Thing, I come up with the same questions. I *know* something was up there, but it couldn't have been there just to terrify me once in a while, surely. What would be the point of that? Did it affect others?

No one I knew ever mentioned it. Mind you, I suppose I never mentioned it to them at the time, or in later years. Also, if it was determined to terrify people (or even just me), why was it living on the top of a church of all places? Indeed, *how* did it live on the top of a church? If it was alive, how and where did it eat and sleep?

As I've got older, I hardly ever think about all of this anymore.

But sometimes I do.

It wouldn't be correct to say *I forgot about it and moved on*. Oh no—I've never forgotten it.

Perhaps The Very Terrible Thing forgot me and moved on.

It made no sense at the time.

It doesn't now.

But that didn't stop it being there for years, every time I walked past.

Reflection

Did this story make you reflect on any of your own similar childhood experiences?

Where Does Anything Start?

Today, at our monthly 'family get-together', my granddaughter told us all that she wants someone to buy her a drum kit. She's eight years old. Why on earth does she want a drum kit?

Who knows why anyone really wants something or chooses to do something? OK, I know some people say, 'From the moment I saw so and so (a rock star, an actor, a sports person, whatever), I knew that was what I wanted to do'. Really...?

Where does any event, occurrence—call it what you will—in life actually 'start'? I don't think you can be certain. Large or small, that event is just part of another series of events. You set out down the road of life, and there are already things on it that affect your path, your direction, the speed you travel, and what you can and can't do. You dodge one thing (or think you do) only to meet something else that stops you going where you *thought* you wanted to get to—or at least changes the path you were going to take to get there.

Or then again, maybe it speeds you up so you get there faster (or somewhere else) than you intended. I vaguely remember a line from studying *Hamlet* for English 'A' Level many years ago. Hamlet says something like, "There's a destiny that shapes our ends, rough-hew them how we will." Our teacher asked us, 'What do you think that means?' I guessed more or less right.

So, does it matter that my granddaughter says she wants to play the drums? We (me, my wife, or/and her mum and dad) could no doubt distract her and probably, hopefully, will distract her. For me, it's not the expense or the noise. For me, it's something else—something that goes way back to when I was 19 at university. 1979.

Back then, not many students visited the university library on a Sunday. In fact, the only reason my friend Jerry and I went there at all was that we both had an important assignment due in on the following Tuesday. Time had caught up with us; neither of us had done much work for our assignment. I was studying economics. Jerry was a modern linguist. We started out with the best of intentions on that Sunday. We'd finally go over there and do the necessary work. Yes, we would. After lunch, obviously. It was hardly going to be an early start, given that it was a Sunday, was it?

This was back in the days long before laptops and the internet. We learned from books in those days. Books. I've always liked books. On weekdays, there used to be quite a few staff in the library reception area, issuing and collecting the books when you produced your library card. Yes. Really.

We had a quick sandwich about 12:00 and (inevitably) a couple of pints in our college's bar before walking across campus to the library. A couple of pints on a largely empty stomach produced a pleasant feeling and may have affected our behaviour. Did it all start with this?

The entrance area on the ground floor of the library was almost completely deserted. There were no other students in sight, and the one member of staff on the entrance desk didn't even look up as we walked in.

We went to the lift, and being slightly affected by the beer, I accidentally pressed the button for the fourth floor instead of the third, which was where the economics books were. I'd only ever been up to the fourth floor once in eighteen months, right at the beginning of my first year on an introductory tour. As I recalled, there weren't many books up there; it was mostly staff offices, other admin, and storage areas.

Now, perhaps this was where 'it all started'. If we'd gone back down to the third floor straight away, things would have been different.

It was really quiet up there, even by Sunday standards. Deserted—and darker too. Being in what obviously was an admin area on a Sunday, most of the lights were not on. Out of vague curiosity, I wandered about ten yards (it was yards in those days) from the lift down the corridor and came across an office which had its door slightly open. The name on it said, 'Ms Debbie de Souza'.

To this day, I have no idea who Ms Debbie de Souza was—and possibly still is—or what role she performed in the library.

Ms de Souza's office had a glass front. Her slightly open door was on the left of a big glass panel, so you could easily see what was inside. On her desk was a book. A large book; very imposing. If you've seen that *Pirates of the Caribbean* film, when the pirates (the actors grossly overacting and obviously having great fun) argue over a passage in the book containing 'The Pirate Code'—it's the scene with Keith Richards in it as Captain Teague. If you've seen it, you'll know what I mean. This book was like that. Huge. Imposing. Significant.

There was no such thing as CCTV back then to make you worry about going into someone's private office. Perhaps if Jerry had been there, he'd have said something to stop me, but he'd wandered off. Later, he told me it was to find a toilet.

There was something about that book that made me want to take a closer look. I can't say exactly what. It appeared old—I mean, very old—and as I pushed open the door and approached it, it had a slightly musty smell.

The book was open, which meant two pages were visible. The text was in Latin, so it made no sense at all to me. I might just about have been able to read a bit of French and have a guess at its meaning, but not Latin. I searched in vain for a word that might look familiar, but no luck.

On one of the pages, there was a diagram beneath two paragraphs of text, and it looked like a drawing of some planets, although it didn't appear to be our solar system. I thought at the time perhaps it was, but given the book's apparent age, it had been drawn before some of the planets had been discovered.

Perhaps it was a history book. I turned over the page—oh, and there was none of that 'the page felt like it would break due to its age' stuff; it was fine. But the next bit was the same: unreadable Latin text and more planets. Perhaps they were actually stars and not planets. I couldn't read it, so I didn't know.

Giving up on that and turning over several more pages, I had obviously entered a different chapter. More Latin, but now there were drawings of animals accompanying the text. Well, I say animals, these all looked like toads—but with much larger eyes and mouths than any I'd ever seen pictured before. The next page had something that looked like an octopus but with more than eight tentacles. Again, it appeared to me to have very odd eyes, much, much too large. In fact, it seemed to have more than two eyes, and if you looked at the drawing in a certain way, it looked like there was an eye at the end of each tentacle.

I say 'looked at it in a certain way' because the picture wasn't completely clear. If the book actually was 'hundreds of years old' (which was the phrase that entered my head), it wasn't surprising that it had faded quite a lot. And the room was only dimly lit. Nevertheless, I was interested. What was that a picture of? Some primeval things from the depths of the ocean? What did I know? Very little. I'd been advised to 'drop' biology as a subject at the age of 14 and 'not to continue the subject to examination level' by my teacher, Mr ('Tadpole') Taylor.

I also recall thinking that, OK, I'd had a chance to look at some mysterious old book that I'd never have seen otherwise, but hey, whatever Ms de Souza was researching, cataloguing, or whatevering, it was never going to make any sense to me.

I ought to be getting on with my economics assignment.

But I didn't. Well, not immediately. Now, perhaps this is where it all really began: my decision to flick through a few more pages of that old book.

One last time.

Another new chapter... and this time it was about musical instruments. Even with a text I couldn't read, I could see that. There was some sort of curved wooden thing, sort of like a recorder—what was the point of that, I thought? It must have been difficult to play. At the bottom of the page was a picture of a drum. Well, a bongo or tom-tom. That sort of thing. I didn't know anything or care about drums and bongos (though I certainly do now), but there was something underneath the picture that seemed to be, even to my non-musical eye, a series of drum notations; rhythmic beats.

Maybe it all started when Jerry finally reappeared and asked what I was looking at.

"Take a look at this, mate," I said, or something like that. "It's to do with drums."

Jerry was a drummer. He was in a college band (which was really good), playing mostly standard rock covers with some original compositions thrown in, and was obsessed with drums and drumming. Back in the 1970s, the government gave you a grant, not a loan, to go and study at university. There was no loan. (I'll say that again: the government gave you money to go to university.) "Three years learning to play the drums on the state!" he used to say. He was always looking to improve his drumming. He looked at the pages I was viewing.

Immediately, whatever he saw made much more sense to him than it did to me.

He stared for a while, looking excited and sort of entranced. After about fifteen seconds of silence, I asked him what he made of it.

I don't remember what I had for lunch two days ago, but what happened in the next couple of minutes in that room is still clear in my head. Even after all this time.

"Wow. It's like... I need to copy this down."

"Copy what down?" I asked.

"This," he said, "it's like woo..." He was clearly very excited, picked up a pen, and started tapping a rhythm on the table.

"Like woo...? What?"

Jerry didn't respond. He seemed deep in thought.

He stared at the page. Long pause—and then he tapped the pen again.

"What is it, mate?" I asked.

"It's like... Yeah, yeah, I get this," he said. "Gotta get these beats down."

I was about to ask again what it all was about and why the beats were so seemingly important, but now I needed to go to the toilet after the beers and asked him where it was.

"Down there on the left," he said vaguely.

When I came back, Jerry had obviously copied some of the book down onto some of Ms de Souza's scrap paper (no mobiles with cameras in those days) and was staring at it with a very distant look on his face. Don't ask me why, but something about him made me suddenly, I don't know exactly... unsettled?

"Let's go," I said. "We've got work to do. We shouldn't be here anyway."

We walked back to the lift, and I pressed the button for the third floor. Jerry pressed 'G' for 'ground'. I shot him a look as if to say, "Aren't you going to the second floor?" which is where he usually went to work. I got out at the third. That was it for the day; I don't know where he went after I got out, but I suspect it wasn't the second floor to do his work.

After that, I didn't see Jerry for ages. We hadn't fallen out or anything like that, but our paths never seemed to cross. It was just that I had, rather belatedly, realised I needed to do some proper studying to try and get on with my degree, so I finally began actually doing some work. He, according to his mates, spent most of his time in one of the music practice rooms that the college had, practising with the band or on his own.

I ran into him one day about two weeks later outside one of the campus' banks. Remember, in those days there were no debit cards. We used cash.

"Jerry! Where've you been?" I asked.

"It all came from that Sunday library visit," he said. That didn't directly answer my question. He must have seen the puzzled look on my face. "That book. Those pages you showed me had a series of weird drumbeats. I can't shake it... shake them. It's like nothing you've ever heard."

I just nodded. Jerry sensed that this still hadn't answered my question.

"Right, ok, ok, follow me. Come with me. Now."

Virtually in silence, although there must have been some talk, but I can't recall it, he more or less dragged me across campus into a practice room that he said he had booked for that morning.

"Listen to this, I mean listen to this."

He then started to play a series of... I don't know... beats? Rhythms? After a minute or so, he showed no sign of stopping and actually seemed to have forgotten that I was there. I'd always hated drum solos and told him so. In a good-natured way, of course.

Booma boomada doomada doomada bumpada bumpada bam bam doompeter. I don't know how else to say it. That, or something like it, repeated many times—and there were other beats as well that I can't now recall. I suppose that for some people it might turn into what is now called an 'earworm'. There was something about it, but I didn't like it at all, both in terms of 'just drums on their own' and the actual sound.

"Gonna do something like this at The Big Gig," he said. This was the open-air gig, or rather a series of gigs, where the college bands put on a show on Midsummer's Day in an area slightly down the hill from the college. The area was apparently going to house a new computing block or something, but nothing had happened so far, and the Students' Union had got permission to use it for a campus festival. Jerry's band was headlining it.

About a week after this enforced listening, I ran into Nigel ('Nige', as he much preferred to be called), who I knew from my Political Economy lectures. We were never exactly friends, but we were on nodding 'you OK?' terms. Nige was the keyboard player in Jerry's band. He knew I knew Jerry.

I made some polite comment about "looking forward to the gig?". I was taken aback when Nige immediately blurted out something along the lines of how difficult things were because Jerry was trying to insist on doing a drum solo in the middle of one particular song.

"Those drumbeats. Those bloody drumbeats," he went on. "We've got a good song, our own composition – you know, the usual 'my life's awful, I hate my job, the system stinks, but I love you, baby'. It's not as crap as that, obviously, but anyway, he now says he wants to do a drum solo in the middle of it, and it just doesn't lend itself to that."

"What's happening then?" I asked.

"Well, in a band, you compromise, and he's a great drummer – but it's not only the solo; he's introduced these new beats to it. It's not that they don't fit as such, but they upset the whole bouncy, 'pop' feel of it. He's done that with some other songs too. Ach, we'll sort it. Like I say, you've got to compromise."

Well, that's 'the story so far'.

Bear with me if you're thinking, 'what's happened to the "where does anything start?" bit?'. Let's move to The Night (of the gig) itself.

What actually happened on that night isn't well documented. That's right, it isn't well documented. Why, you might ask, after what happened?

Let's look at the situation. It was a small college student event, not a massive outdoor festival. There had been two previous similar events in the last two years, which had passed without incident. There had never been any issues with poor behaviour or 'noise upsetting the locals' (who were, in any event, a long way from campus). There was no one 'in authority' around, just members of the Ent's (entertainments) Committee and the Junior College Council, because there was no need.

Jerry's band didn't go on stage until about 10.00 pm, and by then most of the audience had been drinking (and quite possibly taking various substances) for most of the afternoon and evening.

So, they came on. You know, I honestly can't recall now what they were called. (Probably 'The Something or Other'). Great start to the gig. Thirty minutes or so of tight, rocky songs. Covers, and a couple of their own. The audience were really happy. Dancing. Singing.

Then it came to 'that song' – the one that Nige had spoken to me about. Whatever the band had compromised on, Jerry did do his drum solo right after Nige's keyboard break.

He'd nailed the rhythm. Well, I suppose he'd been practicing it for weeks. There it was again: that 'booma boomada' stuff. Powerful, repetitive, loud, hypnotic. Everyone was looking at him. He seemed to sense that, and after a while (no one later could remember exactly how long), he went into a series of almighty, fast, thundering beats on the bass drum while crashing the cymbals. (Keith Moon would have been proud. Go look him up.) Then he stood up behind his kit and took an exaggerated bow.

You could tell that he intended to sit back down and carry on with his solo. You just knew it.

Thank God he didn't. His decision to take a bow and stop those 'booma boomada' beats temporarily is what saved his life. In fact, I suspect it saved many lives that night.

Some said the ground opened up.

Some said, the sky opened up.

Others said both opened up.

Whatever. Something that should not have been opened up did open up.

And what do I mean by that?

Well, it was a long time ago, and I was a fair way away from the stage, struggling towards it while carrying a large number of bottles of beer from the bar for the mates I was with. I was concentrating on not dropping them. It wasn't easy, especially as I'd "had a drink" already, but I wasn't anywhere near drunk.

As I recall, those at the front of the audience were suddenly sucked, dragged, and pulled forward very, very fast towards the stage. They were pulled inexorably towards the... well, 'hole' isn't the right word... void, maybe... that now filled the horizon behind the stage.

There was much screaming from those closest to it, especially from two or three who got 'smashed' into the front of the stage by the force pulling them. This was drowned out by a sort of roar that came from that void. I won't forget it, but it's impossible to describe it accurately. Ever heard the noise hippos make? A very deep 'Uuugh Uurg Uuurg Ug Ug' sound. That was, sort of, it. Following that was a much higher-pitched 'arkle arkle ark arkle ark' sound. Both were produced by God knows what.

There was a smell a bit like an electrical transformer overheating. And something else as well. Not unpleasant as such, but in sharp contrast to the previous warm, clear night air.

A lot of stage gear – amps, spare guitars, leads, etc. – went flying backwards too. So did Jerry's kit, which knocked him sideways to the right. After that, all I can say is it was like someone accidentally turning the master volume control on a sound system in a club up to an extremely loud maximum. Very suddenly. For an instant. At the same time as the lights in the club go out.

Shock.

Then the person in charge realises what they've done and mutes the sound. At the same time, the lights come back on.

I could see the stage was trashed, but there were no more strange noises, smells, or voids – or whatever. Back to normal.

Normal?

Micky, the guitarist, who had turned to look at Jerry taking his bow, appeared to have been snatched (is the word I'd have to use) backwards by something (although nothing was visible to me), and for a moment seemed to disappear. But he'd actually smashed into a lighting rig. His guitar, or the strap, caught against it, and he managed somehow to grab the rig as he was swung around. His position was such that he was looking into the void. I was too far away to see what he was staring at, but from what I could see of his face, he looked terrified.

He collapsed right there on what was left of the stage and was taken to hospital. Who called 999 or how, I don't know – as I said, this was long before mobile phones. He never recovered. It's said that he never spoke again. In fact, it's said that he never really did anything again – never recognised anyone, never tried to get up from his bed, never fed himself or whatever. His mind and brain had gone. Friends visited for a while, but apparently, he'd become catatonic, and they stopped going. He passed away, peacefully, we were told, three months later.

Jerry wasn't in that sort of extreme state, although he went to hospital too that night – he had to. He was obviously also in very deep shock. Not as bad as Micky, maybe because he was mostly facing away from the stage and never saw clearly whatever it was that Micky saw. But something had affected him; after all, he was closest to whatever it was that was behind him.

He wasn't like Micky, but he was still changed forever. When I visited him in hospital a couple of days later, he was curious about things in a naïve, childlike manner. "Where do clouds come from?", "Why do numbers go on forever?", "Why can't animals talk?" were just three of the things he asked me. We were sitting outside his ward in the sun on a terrace. I used to smoke in those days, and hospitals, while discouraging smoking, weren't anything like they are these days. He asked if I had got a cigarette. I gave him one, and he smoked it right down to the filter. Thirty seconds later, he asked, "You got a cigarette?" That just repeated until I ran out of cigarettes.

He was clearly in absolutely no condition to continue his studies, and it was decided by his parents and the college (I doubt if he had any input into this) that he should 'take a year out'.

A year? He never came back. I never saw him or heard from him again.

You are probably thinking, 'Didn't the university authorities look into it?' Yes – and no. The Master of College, who didn't like being contacted in the evening, was called. Of course he was, doubtless much to his annoyance, but by the time he arrived, most people had gone. I certainly had. As far as I am aware, the police weren't called.

Any valuable items of stage gear had been removed – the consensus amongst the organisers was that 'whatever happened, we'll sort the dismantling of the stage tomorrow'. Apparently, there were a few people still sitting around, but they were either too stunned, stoned, or both to make much, if any, sense. The Master went home, apparently saying something about 'calling the hospital right away and having an investigation in the morning'.

Now, I vaguely recall a questionnaire being circulated to students asking if they were there and what they saw, if they were, but I don't think there were that many responses. It wasn't 'hushed up', but in the days that followed, people just didn't want to talk about the event and what they'd seen or thought they'd seen. I imagine the university didn't want any awkward publicity and so perhaps weren't as inquisitive as they might have been. There was some vague reference in the local paper about 'several injured at college concert' (rather than 'gig') and that was more or less the proverbial 'it'. You won't find anything online if you look. I know, I've already tried.

That's my recollection of that night. All those years ago. Probably some details aren't quite right, and no doubt my descriptions sound odd (or implausible), but that's the best I can do.

In my mind, I'm pretty sure of what happened. And why it happened, but not how it all came about.

You know that thing where an opera singer can shatter a wine glass by singing a particular note? Well, just because there's a wine glass and someone singing a particular note, that doesn't mean the glass will shatter. It has to be the right note, the right pitch (or whatever), held for a particular time, a particular distance from the glass, and probably a particular type of glass, etc. etc. But it can happen.

Some things cause others.

Back to the start. I suppose we could easily stop my granddaughter playing the drums, but then she might decide to be a singer instead – and therefore be able to shatter the glass. The glass is there to be shattered. And could be shattered if certain events transpire.

In case you were wondering, I don't know what happened to Nige or the rest of the band. But there was certainly no more Jerry as he used to be. Maybe he 'got better'. I don't know, but I doubt it.

Obviously, there was no more Micky.

Where did 'No More Jerry and No More Micky' actually start?

And could it happen to my granddaughter?

You tell me.

Reflection

What is the central theme of this story?

At what point did the theme of the story start? Where did it end?

An Important Meeting

God wasn't happy. There was too much nastiness throughout creation. Too much cruelty. Too much neglect. Most of the religions that had sprung up across the universe since time began now had little to do with what they had originally set out to achieve. It wasn't what had been planned.

A meeting had been called with some of the archangels and saints to discuss the situation.

"Right; you all know why we are here," said God.

Everyone did, but no one wanted to speak first.

Eventually, Saint Paul said, rather hesitantly, "Look, you've always told us we could speak frankly."

"Yes. Yes," said God, who sounded distinctly tetchy. That was noted by everyone; it wasn't an auspicious start.

Saint Paul—although not an angel—had a very deep understanding of the issues, having, as someone had once put it, *"worked firsthand in the field,"* which was the reason he was at the meeting.

"Well, you are omniscient; you must have seen this coming."

It was a good question and not one that any of the archangels looked like they would have been comfortable asking, even if they had been thinking along the same lines.

God shot him something of a sharp look. Paul was a trusted lieutenant, but the look suggested that this particular level of frankness wasn't necessarily welcome.

"And... and therefore," said Saint Paul quickly, picking up on this and never having seen *The Boss* in such a mood, "you obviously know what to do to sort it out."

"Look," said God, "there's omniscience and there's *omniscience*. The whole of creation—with everything always changing, every sentient being, never mind the non-sentient ones, making choices the whole time... I can get most of it—"

(Considerable nodding in agreement from the group—after all, there could be no doubt about that.)

"But *all* of it. *All* the time?"

No one said anything.

God had always encouraged the angels to visit creation—the whole vastness of it. When they did, they took on an appropriate appearance on the chosen planet, lived a normal life while never forgetting why they were there, and then reported back when their visit—or 'life'—ended. It was one thing being (mostly) omniscient at a distance, but it was always good to hear things firsthand from someone who had actually been there.

Sadly, God reflected, the reporting back—and the articulating of ideas resulting from these visits—meant that, no doubt as a result of 'going native' for a while, there was now a particular way of speaking and expressing a view. Oddly, even allowing for millions of different languages and cultures, this had occurred all across creation and resulted in a similar style of delivering an opinion.

"As I see it, we need a simple restatement of the fundamental issues," said Gabriel.

This was just the sort of comment that made God's eyes roll. God, obviously, couldn't say *Oh God* (but sometimes wished such a thing was possible), and so tended to say "Ah, Me"—and did so, very quietly, at this point.

There was silence again.

Then the Archangel Raphael spoke up.

"Let's get radical here."

(God's eyes rolled again.)

"I mean, this 'without faith I am nothing' bit. Why not just demonstrate a *'Hello! Here I am!'* approach? This wouldn't be a threat, obviously—certainly not—just an attempt to say… like, *'I'm here and watching over everything, including you, so think on. Be nice.'*"

Further silence while this was considered.

"Look, we've got history on our side here," Raphael continued. "Jesus let them kill him and then rose from the dead three days later. That's a bit of a giveaway that he was actually *someone*—"

(He placed emphasis on that word.)

"—i.e., somebody who is rather different. It was very much a definite 'look what can happen if you follow me'. The prophets weren't making all that much progress, so he went ahead and spelled it out."

"Not everybody bought into that, as you well know," said Archangel Michael. "And have you read Orwell's *1984*? *Big Brother is watching you*, etc."

Raphael, who had absorbed every work of literature, art and everything else from all across creation, responded immediately.

"Yes, yes, but… no, no, obviously not like that. We manage it carefully. I'm just saying—"

(He bowed to God)

"—show you exist. You know… *I'm God, there is an afterlife*, and then they'll realise that doing, er, good stuff will get them to the, er, right place. I.e., here."

Raphael had the feeling he hadn't made his case as clearly as he might have.

"I've some sympathy with that view," said Archangel Uriel. "But the problem as I see it is—how would that be achieved? I mean, if you—"

(He nodded very deferentially to God)

"—appeared on a planet's communication systems, how would you appear? What shape? Form? Sex? What apparent gender would you be?"

He paused.

"I suppose you could be an indistinct but obviously powerful, welcoming, glowing white light sort of being. Most cultures like glowing white light," he finished, somewhat lamely.

"As you really ought to know, I can appear however I want to all the different planets, peoples, cultures and, where they exist, religions," said God, with some asperity. "All across the universe. At the same time."

"Ah," broke in Saint Paul. "But on any particular planet, one lot would say something like *'the true God from our religion wouldn't also appear as someone else looking like blah blah from another religion'*. And the other lot—or lots—would say the same."

"I'm *always* the true God. The real deal," said God, who promptly realised that particular choice of words was a mistake, as it encouraged the others to speak in a similar manner.

"There are many roads to me. Why can't they see that without all this bitterness? *Why?!*"

"Omniscience," muttered Saint Paul rather too loudly—and got another sharp look.

"There's another issue here," said Uriel. "Most of them would claim the communication device you appeared on had been—"

(Here he paused, apparently thinking of the correct word)

"—*hacked*, and that it wasn't you at all."

"Appear in the sky of a planet rather than through… what's it called… social media?" mused God aloud. "Across the whole of creation, every planet. Perhaps it is time for a grand entrance. Or maybe in people's minds?"

"Same issue as before, as what?" said Uriel. "And I'm not sure about in minds. Our detractors would say it was a collective hallucination or some sort of mental illness."

"For everyone to see me, it would have to be a mighty 'hallucination'," said God. "Surely, they'd realise that. And that's the point… I mean, if everyone saw me, then whatever they thought, they'd have to pay attention."

"You'd have to think very carefully about what you'd say," said Raphael. "You might convince a large number, but suppose most of them started panicking, thinking 'The End' had come. It might trigger all sorts of chaotic events."

"Yes, yes, I've thought of that. I'm not going to just go 'Hello, I'm God, but no need to panic because I've not come to announce the apocalypse, just to tell you that you need to behave better.' I'd say more than that."

"Well, that's actually not bad for an opening gambit," said Raphael, "but sadly most sentient beings don't like to listen to long speeches anymore. It'd have to be a series of... clever soundbites."

"Ah, me," muttered God. "Clever soundbites..."

"And just being pragmatic," broke in Gabriel, "if you did it in the day, on any given planet, then obviously somewhere it's nighttime; half the population would be asleep. You'd have to do a second sitting."

"OK, scrub that," said Uriel. "What about 'one-on-one' visits with the great and the good... and great and not so good?"

"Tried it already," said God. "A disaster, at least most of the time. No, Paul"—he turned to the saint—"don't mention omniscience again, I know you're thinking about it."

Saint Paul shifted uncomfortably in his chair and looked rather embarrassed.

"What happens when I appear is usually, 'Who are you? How did you get in here?' They put my majestic appearance and presence—tailored to their culture and belief, obviously—down to a dream, or an illusion caused by some sort of drug they must have taken. I say something like, 'I know all about you and your schemes and I want to speak to you about changing your ways.'

"They then go, 'Well, you can get all that nonsense about me off the internet,' or whatever it is they have on the planet. Then they try to call security, which I've already prevented, obviously. So, they tend to panic and are then not the slightest bit amenable to rational debate. Loads of times I've had a gun pulled on me. Although, naturally, I wasn't bothered by that."

Further silence followed this revelation.

"It really is a non-runner," God continued. "The supposedly religious ones can't accept the possibility that they might be wrong. I'm, apparently, the fraud in their eyes! I find that profoundly depressing, since usually religions started out with the best of intentions.

"The ruthless dictators are mad and paranoid. I've long discovered that in neither case is a change of heart going to happen. They will never go out to their people, admit they got it all wrong, ask for understanding and forgiveness, and say that from henceforth they should all behave nicely, be sensible, be… oh… well, you see what I'm saying."

"You say they pulled a gun?" asked Saint Paul in a tone that suggested he had just had a good idea. "We know the old instruction, 'Do not put God to the test', but times have changed. Well, if they shot at you, you could show that you weren't affected and that you were who you said you were. That ought to convince them."

"Look. I'm well and truly done with appearing to lunatic leaders across creation in the middle of the night!" said God irritably. "And as for offering them the opportunity to kill me so that I can prove them wrong…"

Saint Paul could see he had made a mistake.

"Now a very radical approach would be the whole free will thing," Saint Peter spoke up for the first time. He thought deeply about these matters but was hardly ever the first to contribute to a discussion. "I don't mean abolish it completely but…"

"Don't go there," said God. "It's too late for changes like that. I can't wipe everyone's mind and reprogram the whole universe. I know the argument—in fact, I thought about it for ages before time even began—about setting up creation so that certain unpleasant, nasty… whatever-you-want-to-call-them situations couldn't exist, so that beings could not behave in a particular way.

"But that's not what the plan was. I—*we*," the word was emphasised pointedly while looking at all of the archangels simultaneously, "decided to set it all up according to certain laws. I—*we*—can tinker here and there, which is what you lot should have been doing on your visits, but we can't alter the fundamentals. It's what holds it all together."

Silence again. Then Saint James finally spoke up.

"Now might be the time to say that I have it on good authority that 'The Opposition' are not happy," he said with a positive tone in his voice. "For precisely the opposite reason why we are all here in this meeting. The pace of what we might colloquially call 'all the bad stuff happening' hasn't gone anywhere nearly as fast as they planned across creation.

"Now while we are naturally—and rightly—concerned because it is undeniable that they have had some successes, some on a very grand scale, on an individual level, which is where they hoped the big gains would be, these haven't occurred in anything like the numbers expected. The word is that they aren't meeting any of their targets."

"I've been following that too. In many parts of creation, doctors are giving them pills and therapy," chipped in Raphael. "They're being told, 'This idea of an actual evil force is all in your mind,' and any contact with one of their foot soldiers gets put down to some sort of mental illness. They are being medicalised out of relevance!"

"The information I have from The Backchannels is that 'You Know Who' isn't a—oh, what was the phrase? Oh yes—*happy bunny*."

Notwithstanding the seriousness of the situation, the application of that particular phrase to that particular entity made most of them smile.

"Always beats me why they bother at all," said Michael. "I mean, they know that when The End comes—since you," he nodded deferentially to God, "created them in the first place—that you are therefore the more powerful. You caused them to come into existence because of your power, and they chose to work against you. They're never going to win. Crazies. The lot of 'em."

"Off their heads," Uriel spoke up in agreement. "But I suppose once you've been daft enough to nail your colours to *that* particular mast, that's it. If you weren't insane before you joined—hah!—you would be afterwards. Off their heads," he repeated.

"But very wicked and dangerous with it," Michael reminded them (although they hardly needed reminding). "They need to be, ah, *dealt with*. Unless they truly repent, of course," he added rather hastily.

"Perhaps that's their rationale," Uriel continued. "'We're going to lose, so we might as well cause as much trouble as we can while we're still here.'"

"Well, at least that's some good news," said Raphael.

"Well, it's not good enough," said God firmly. "And reviewing their progress—or the lack of it—is not why we are here. Now isn't the time for this sort of philosophical discussion."

There was a very long silence this time. There were many deep thoughts.

"What are we to do then?" asked God.

Saint Thomas Aquinas, who was very well respected, spoke up for the first time.

"Press 'reboot'?"

"Ah, me," said God. "Thomas, you are one of the great thinkers of the universe, but in this case you haven't thought it through at all."

Thomas looked a bit puzzled.

"What about the lot that are already here in heaven with us?" prompted Saint Peter, who knew exactly what God meant. "You know… those waiting for their loved ones to get here?"

"Well," said Thomas smoothly, "they all have the right characteristics and frame of mind to be here, obviously—or, er, they wouldn't be here in the first place. So, they won't be bothered. I believe a much-used phrase is *they will be cool with that*."

Gabriel broke in rather bluntly. "Right characteristics or not, I think you're underestimating how"—he adopted a rather sarcastic storytelling tone—"Old Jeff up here, who was married to his beloved Dotty for sixty years and is looking forward to seeing her again shortly, is going to react to being told that, in fact, it's not going to happen because we've decided to start creation all over again. Just saying," he added with an embarrassed cough, while looking at Saint Peter for support, seeing the looks he was getting.

"We can't start creation again anyway. We all knew that from before time started," said God.

"Well, I wasn't around then," said Thomas, slightly defensively.

God didn't want to say something like *yes, but you might have worked it out by now*, and being kindly, simply said, "Anyway, that's the way it is. So, I'll ask again—what are we going to do about the way things are out there?"

"Answer more prayers. A bit quicker?" said Uriel.

"Well, I'm not exactly shirking that," replied God, in a tone similar to the one used when referring to visiting dictators in the night. "I never stop. But you all know how careful you have to be with answering prayers. Alter one thing—one small thing—for a very worthy *ask*, and it can cause huge ructions elsewhere.

"Also"—God sighed at this point—"I don't mind hearing a prayer for help about someone's illness or asking for forgiveness; obviously, I welcome those. But, ah me, a lot of it these days is stuff like asking for their team to avoid relegation or stopping their fish pond in the garden from leaking."

There was, again, silence while this was absorbed.

"At least they are praying. It shows they believe you exist and that you care for creation," said Raphael smoothly. "That's a good sign."

"True. Yes. Well, I suppose I could delegate a bit more of the answering to you lot." Heads nodded in agreement.

God paused, ruefully muttered something inaudible about fish ponds, and then continued, "Well, that's given me a lot to think about, on top of everything else. Thank you all."

The other participants at the meeting nodded deferentially and all disappeared.

God sat alone, very self-absorbed, musing aloud on the points made at the meeting—so much so that Jesus was able to walk in completely unnoticed.

"Who are you talking to?" he asked pleasantly.

"As I'm the most intelligent person around here, I sometimes think it's a good idea to talk to myself," said God.

"Well, so do I!" said Jesus. "Great minds think alike. Actually, it's just occurred to me—aren't our thoughts and conversations where that phrase originated from in the first place? Anyway, look, I've got some ideas about what you've just been talking about from my recent travels."

"Oh yes?" said God, in an interested *go on then, tell me* tone of voice.

"Oh yes indeed," replied Jesus. "You know," he added in a jokey, winding-up tone, "you ought to get out more."

"Yes, but it's always so busy here, and although I'm timeless, I'm getting on a bit," sighed God. It was a line that had been used many times before down the millennia, but Jesus smiled at it anyway—as he always did.

"You're right though, I suppose I should."

"That's the spirit," said Jesus.

Reflection

What points are being made in this story?
Are they valid?

Questions

The first person I saw after I died was David Bowie. He was dressed just like I had seen him on one of his late 1980s tours: sharp and smart. I had no idea why—seeing him first, I mean, not why he was dressed the way he was.

I'd always wanted to ask him questions, like you always want to ask famous people questions. I'd always liked him; who didn't/doesn't? I mean, back in the day, or rather late at night, you could always put on a Bowie album, any album, and know what you'd get.

But I digress a bit. There he was, like me, in this sort of circle or bubble of… not exactly light, but something like it. I was thinking that now he was right in front of me, I could ask some of 'those' questions, you know, the ones you always wanted to ask people like him. But I didn't have to ask him anything, because he answered the question I was going to ask before I could ask it. Just thinking I might ask it, I then got the answer.

That's the only way I can describe the situation. He didn't actually face me directly and speak. No, I just knew the answer to the question I'd thought of asking but never did, because I didn't need to. He'd already told me.

If that's not clear, then you wait until you die and see Bowie.

What were these questions I wanted to ask that got answered even though I didn't get to ask? I can remember the first one, but not the others. And there were others. 'Is it true you said you never made much money from touring?' Before I 'asked', he said, and I sensed that he gave that smile of his, "Obviously I made money from some tours, but it was always very expensive, and it was never as much as you might think.

I know what you are thinking. Bowie! Weren't there about ten million people all surrounding him, wherever we were, asking their questions—or like me, not asking questions but still getting answers? No, there weren't. He wasn't being mobbed; it wasn't like I was at the back of some huge stadium or open-air gig with tens of thousands in front of me, desperately trying to see the man on the stage. But there were loads nearby. I just knew. Perhaps there were millions. Actually, when I say 'nearby', it wasn't like we'd usually use that word. They were there, but 'there' wasn't like 'there' in the usual "up close to" sense; it wasn't 'crowded', but huge numbers of people were definitely there. Could I hear the questions they were asking? No.

The next person I noticed, I also recognised at once. And then I didn't. This person was both a child that I once knew and then a man that I had never seen before—changing between one and the other.

Yes, I immediately recognised a person I knew from school when I was about 14. I hadn't thought about him for 40 years. Joel Barrington-Stone. He'd died in a car crash. Terrible accident. He wasn't a close friend, but nevertheless, I recalled that day in school assembly when it was announced. It was something very sad to be told out of the blue one morning when you were young. Or at any time, I suppose. At the time, I just remembered thinking, 'I'll never play football with him on the field again.'

Then, like with Bowie, before I had the chance to ask the question—one that I'd often thought about—the answer arrived. The question this time was going to be, 'When you die as a child, do you stay as a child in the afterlife (assuming there is one and we are in it), or do you grow up?' "You grow up, you daft sod," (I suddenly remembered that those last three words had been his favourite phrase) "but it's a different type of growing up."

All around me, stretching everywhere, were figures in these 'lights'.

I was taking all this in when one brighter than the others appeared. I just *knew*, somehow—don't ask why or how—that there was a being? in it that 'worked' there and wasn't like the others. The others who were like me, I mean. i.e., dead.

The being exuded calmness and a friendly demeanour. There are no doubt better words that could describe him, her, it? Fill them in yourself if you want.

"Is this heaven?" I asked. (Well, wouldn't you?)

"No, but you've done well to get here. To this point."

"Not everyone gets here?"

"No, they don't. But (and for some reason, at this point, I just knew the rest of the response had been given many times before—millions, hundreds of millions of times) it's a step in the right direction."

"How long will I be here? Will I get to heaven?"

"That depends."

"On what?"

"On you. It could be quite a long time because 'getting to heaven' may not be quite what you think it means."

"A long time? Surely there's no time here, is there?" I asked—ignoring the second part of what had just been said, although afterwards, I realised it was the more significant part.

"Well," (this word was spoken in a rather drawn-out manner) "there is—and there isn't."

That actually made sense to me.

"What's the next step after this then?"

I didn't get a straight answer. "The important thing is to deal with and concentrate on this situation for now. You have to…" (there was a pause, even though I thought this also must have been asked multiple millions of times before) "…master this step first. And how long it takes depends on you."

"How do I know what I should do?"

"You'll know, you'll develop. Through interacting with others." There was a very nice, positive tone being used, and I liked it. I suppose I should have known I was going to get an answer like that (although, hang on, I'd never been dead before, so how would I know?). I decided to ask a different question.

"What happens to those who don't make it here?"

"Put it this way," (yet again, there was that sense of a prepared answer coming) "some of them..."

Boom! Bang! (Or maybe just a massive 'Pow!!', whatever.) The next thing I knew, I was alive again, back in the hospital, but with a terrible pain in my chest, gasping for air, and feeling the worst I'd ever felt.

Like death warmed up.

I was dizzy and confused. I was in a room on my own, not on a ward, with a doctor in front of me saying something about "...the defibrillator... quite a while ago... just checking on you... making sure you are OK." I had no idea how long after they restarted my heart it was.

The doctor looked about 18 to me (well, that's what happens when you get old, isn't it?) but she was adopting a professional manner. Was she properly qualified? Was she a student? I didn't really care. I was alive—wasn't I? I remember thinking that if I still noticed such things, that was encouraging.

"And… I'm OK?" I didn't know what else to say, or rather croak.

"You made it," she replied, smiling.

"So, I died?"

"Your heart stopped. Yes."

"But there was still oxygen in my brain?"

"Yes."

"But not as much as normal?"

"That's right."

"Could my brain have been damaged?"

"We will be doing more tests, but from your physical reactions and how you are talking to me now, that doesn't seem to be the case." She smiled in a reassuring way. I appreciated that.

"I saw something. A sort of vision," I blurted out.

She nodded, not exactly gravely, but certainly sombrely.

"Do you want to know what I saw?"

She looked straight at me. "A glowing white light at the end of a tunnel? Relatives there to greet you?" It was mildly inquisitive and wasn't asked in a sarcastic tone. I appreciated that too.

"Well, not exactly, but yes, sort of." (I didn't want to mention David Bowie.)

"Would you like me to get the chaplain to come along? I saw from your notes you are Church of England."

"Well, nominally," I said. "I've never thought of myself as being particularly religious until…" I paused.

"Now?" she finished. "I know where she'll be at this hour. I'll drop by her office and ask her to come over."

I nodded. "Have people said this sort of thing to you before? I mean, situations like this. The white light. Is that what you've been told—or taught?" I think I sounded a bit desperate, but the situation was what it was.

"I've been a doctor for two years and I've heard of situations like yours occurring, but I'll be honest, I've never personally had a patient of mine say they have had... what did you say? 'A vision'."

She didn't seem keen to discuss this any further and said that, as I seemed to be 'making progress' or some such, and that if I didn't need anything at the moment, she would need to be off to see her other patients but that I would be checked on regularly. Blah, blah. Nevertheless, I muttered my thanks and dozed off.

What followed went as follows. I woke up—or drifted into consciousness, or whatever—and I heard a voice. There was a lady standing by my bed.

"Mr Roberts? I've called in because I heard that you've had an... (there was a very slight pause)... experience."

I had actually briefly wondered what the hospital's lady chaplain might be like; young and full of modern theories (whatever they might be) and enthusiasm about God, or an older, more staid, 'traditional' type full of what I suppose you might call 'the usual platitudes.' She was neither, appearing about 45 and speaking... well, what follows shows how she was speaking.

"Yes," was all I could think of to say.

"I know some of the details, but… tell me about it."

"Well, when I died, at least I think I died, or whatever happened, I think I went somewhere. I didn't see anyone I knew. Or, well, I did see someone actually, but... but certainly not my parents or anyone I was close to that has died."

"That doesn't always happen." She sounded sure about that.

"But is that what usually happens? Should I have seen them?" I was suddenly talking quickly, and I wanted answers. The answer did come rapidly, in fact, immediately.

"When a person dies suddenly, their family, or close friends can't always be there to greet them."

"But they were there?"

There was a slight polite shrug of the shoulders. "Well, there are several possibilities; either they were and didn't get to you before you came back here, or they had been there previously but they had 'moved on'." I realised later I should have asked about that statement, but I was concentrating on the one word she used after 'moved on'. That word was another 'or'—followed by a pause in the conversation which I was clearly supposed to fill. Which I did.

"You mean 'or they never got there in the first place'?"

"Exactly."

"But what is, I mean was, wherever it was I went?"

Again, a very prompt response.

"I always say to someone to think of it as a building with several different levels. And you have a personal lift which means you are able to move up between its floors. Most people go in at the ground floor, as you did, but there are also entrances on the basement level. There's also a sub-basement level."

"But I can't just press the 'up' button."

A wry smile. "No. But your lift will be able to go up when the time is right."

"Can people in the basement go up?" I surprised myself by asking. I don't think, in fact I knew, I'd never had this sort of conversation before.

"That's possible. And I can guess your next question. It is very difficult for those who entered in the sub-basement to move up. Their lift is pretty much stuck."

"They are... in hell?"

"That's a convenient word."

"Burning in fire?"

"I think it's more of a mental issue."

"But they are stuck for eternity? I mean total eternity (I didn't really know how to say what I was thinking). They never get forgiven. Not ever?"

"I don't know the mind or mercy of God. Who does?"

"But you've got a better acquaintance with God than me though, haven't you?" I said, with all the exasperation I could muster, given my state.

"Some people have done the most terrible things," she said, her voice dropping. "You don't need me to tell you that."

"Yes, but... there forever?"

"The effect of what they have done can cause a lot of dreadful repercussions for a lot of others for a long time. A very, very long time. As I said, I don't know the mind of God."

"I suppose so," I said. I suddenly felt very tired. I felt I'd fired all the verbal theological bullets I could think of for the time being. "Thank you anyway. Could you call back at some point?"

"I'm actually going away for a while," she said. "But I hope what I've said has been useful."

"It's certainly given me something to think about," I replied. This sounded a bit stilted, but I didn't know what else to say. Suddenly, another thought occurred to me. "Oh, one more thing." (One more theological bullet got loaded and fired.) "What about people who aren't Church of England or even Christians? What about Jews or Muslims and all the others? Are they there too, in the same place? And... (This really, really was going to be my last bullet) I only saw humans there. What about aliens? We can't be the only ones like us in the universe, and they must go somewhere...."

That was it. I felt tired, drained, and half expected one of the monitors I was linked up to go into alarm mode. Certainly, the white lines on them seemed to be less flat than before. One or two seemed to be spiking alarmingly.

"A very good question. Like I said, think of it as a building with different levels," she replied. "Several levels. And each level has a number of different rooms." And although she didn't, if she'd tapped her nose in a 'you know what I mean' manner, I wouldn't have been the slightest bit surprised.

"What's at the top?" I asked. "If it's heaven, what's it like?"

"Well, I've never been there. Someday, hopefully," was the reply in a slightly joking manner.

"Thank you," I said, feeling very drowsy.

"Just doing my job," she said with a smile, getting up to leave. "You get some rest now." She walked out. I remember seeing the clock. It was 3:15 p.m.

The next time I saw the clock, it was when I was woken up at 4:37 p.m. by someone entering the room.

"Mr Roberts?" a voice asked. "I'm Marcia Littlewood, the hospital chaplain. (She looked the older, staid type). I gather you wanted to speak to me."

I really didn't know how to answer.

Would you?

Reflection

What is the central point of this story?

Lucky Monday

The word 'lucky' featured large in Martin's life. Throughout his early years, he caught all the usual childhood diseases – mumps, measles, and all the rest – but was never seriously ill. He clearly recalled the occasion when he was about seven years old and ill with the same something or other that most of his primary school class had caught. Old Mrs Featherstone, their neighbour, had called round to ask whether "little Martin was alright because it's nasty and there's a lot of it about." He didn't remember what 'it' was, but he did remember that his mother had replied, "Luckily he hasn't been too badly affected."

When it came to his transition to secondary school, Martin got to attend the one he wanted. He had really liked what he had seen of it on the open evening. His parents were pleased too and told him that he was lucky to be there. It was highly regarded for all the right reasons and was an easy bus ride from his home.

There were lots of lucky events like this in his young life.

When someone said that he was lucky, it wasn't said in the way that a parent might say, "Eat your cabbage (or something else you hated) – you're lucky to have it. There are plenty of starving children in the world." A comment like "You are lucky, Martin" (in whatever context) was always well-meant and genuine. He never took it literally, of course, but the comments stayed in his mind. Martin had been particularly impressed by a comment that his history teacher at his new school had made about Napoleon when they were studying his battles. "I'd rather have a lucky general than a good one." He had looked it up, and Napoleon had apparently said something like that.

Aged 13, Martin still looked forward to visiting his grandparents. He and his parents visited them every two weeks or so, usually at the weekend. His grandmother always said how lucky her daughter was to have such a nice son, and the last time they had visited, she had, somewhat bizarrely (although she was 84), actually called Martin 'Lucky' instead of using his proper name.

That was on the Sunday.

On the Monday, Martin woke up feeling very positive. He could see through the curtains in his bedroom that the sun was shining. He didn't have to go to school because it was a teacher training day.

That meant he could avoid an issue that had been troubling him for the last seven months – the unwanted attentions of Danny Hamilton. These attentions did not make him feel lucky.

Martin was in Year 9 and in denial that he was being bullied by Danny, who was in Year 11. But that is patently what it was. There had been several assemblies recently in school focusing on 'its zero tolerance of bullying,' and Martin knew that he should really report what was happening. But he hadn't.

Even after all that had happened, Martin was still at the stage where he felt he could say something to his Form Tutor, his Head of Year, or his parents, but didn't want to. It wasn't that bad (he told himself), and it wasn't as if Danny singled him out. Oh no, he certainly wasn't the only one who was bullied. But the fact was that every time Danny saw him, he would call out something unpleasant. This was usually a variation on "Hi, you worthless piece of shit," followed by a loud, scornful laugh which was echoed by any members of his gang that happened to be with him. There was also the occasional hard punch to the arm or chest in passing. Actually, it had progressed from 'occasional' to 'more or less every time they met,' and increasingly, some of Danny's mates punched him too. Danny had targeted him from the start of the year. Martin had no idea why. He wasn't one to seek confrontation with anyone, still less with someone two years older and much larger than him. Like anyone considering reporting bullying, he feared the bully's reprisal.

The worst days of the week were Monday and Thursday. Period 3. Then, he had English, and his class's room, 'English 4,' was right next to Danny's class in 'English 5'. It was therefore highly likely that before the lesson (when his teacher Miss Davies made them line up outside) or afterwards, in the inevitable scrum in the corridor to get out of the building to the canteen as it was now break, something would occur. Sometimes just a comment from Danny, usually a comment and a punch. Very rarely, nothing. That was the worst part for Martin: not knowing. Monday and Thursday mornings were not 'good'. He didn't feel lucky then. And, of course, he might run into Danny at other times as well.

Nevertheless, Martin kept trying to convince himself that he actually wasn't too upset by the situation. He knew that others throughout the school had attracted far more than verbal abuse, and a punch from Danny, who tried his best to provoke a fight, would be ruthlessly violent if anyone responded and then claim he was simply defending himself. He also knew, as almost everyone in the Lower and Middle School did, of Danny's requests to 'borrow some money'. Money which, needless to say, never got repaid. Luckily, Danny had never approached him for that reason.

On that Monday, Martin had arranged to meet some friends at 10.30 in the park to play football. It was only about half a mile from his house, so he walked. "See you for lunch," he called cheerfully to his mother as he left.

By the entrance to the park was a row of old cottages; 'Railway Cottages 1895' – although needless to say, the adjacent railway line was long gone. They were in a decrepit state and were going to be knocked down. Martin vaguely remembered there had been something in the local news about them. They were council houses, and the last person still living there, in number eight (the one nearest to the park gate), old Mr Potterton? Patterson? had stubbornly refused to move to new accommodation. At 96 years old, he had become something of a local celebrity. The impasse hadn't actually lasted very long because he had died.

The cottages were now surrounded by metal fencing, preventing anyone from reaching them, but the panel that was obviously the gate into the site was wide open on that Monday. There were two large skips close by, filled with various old pieces of building material – wood, bricks, and glass. In one of them, Martin saw something shining. Reflecting the sun quite powerfully, it actually made him dip his head slightly to avoid the glare. What was that? Probably a broken mirror, he told himself.

Curiosity got the better of him. No one was around nearby, either by the cottages or in the park, and the skip itself was only a very short distance away. He darted into the fenced-off area, but as he approached the skip, the sun went behind a cloud, the shining stopped, and where he thought he'd seen it, he couldn't spot anything that might have been the cause of it. What he did see there, among the rubbish, was a grey metal tube, a bit like a small thin thermos flask. It had some writing on it. It obviously hadn't been the source of the reflected shining light, but it looked interesting. He picked it up and trotted back into the park.

There was no sign of his friends yet, so he sat down on a bench close to the football pitches and examined what he had found. Originally, there had obviously been some lettering in red printed on the side of the tube, but it had become so rubbed away over time that it was illegible. The only thing that could be seen fairly clearly was 'XP50'.

A thermos called XP50? With no sign of his friends yet, he got out his phone and googled it. There it was, straight away. On Wikipedia.

"The XP50 was produced in the USA for use in the Vietnam War. It was a hybrid weapon with a ten-second fuse, which was designed to be used either as a hand grenade or an explosive charge. It first saw service in 1971 but was never popular with the troops, who largely regarded it as neither one weapon nor the other. Additionally, it quickly gained a reputation for being unreliable. The firing mechanism was more complicated than that of an ordinary hand grenade, and it attracted the ironic joke that 'XP50' was an abbreviation of 'explodes 50% of the time.' A modification was made to the fuse in 1973, but reports vary as to how effective this actually was, and it remained unpopular and untrusted. Officers in some infantry units even refused to issue it to their troops. Production was discontinued, and the weapon was withdrawn in the summer of 1974."

Here was a picture of it too, and the writing, which had all but disappeared from his XP50, was now clear. In bold red lettering, it stated, 'Unscrew cap. Discard. Press red button down until an audible 'click' is heard. Detonation will occur in approximately ten seconds.'

A number of thoughts went through his mind very quickly. How had a weapon more than fifty years old from the other side of the world found its way into a skip full of junk in England? Maybe the old man had collected military memorabilia? Or it could be a replica. Plenty of people owned replica war stuff. If it was real, then surely there had to be regulations about soldiers leaving the army with a live weapon. But if Mister whoever it was had been in the British army, he wouldn't have fought in Vietnam all that time ago, would he?

It couldn't be real.

But it looked real. It felt real. It was quite heavy for its size. If it had been a weapon once and somehow fashioned into a thermos, wouldn't it be lighter?

Some loud, unpleasant laughter broke his train of thought and snapped Martin back into his present situation. He knew that laugh – Danny.

Not just Danny. He was accompanied by Alan Lucas. Alan, who had long greasy hair and bad acne, was effectively Danny's 'number 2'. Martin had been so distracted he hadn't been aware of their approach. His mind had vaguely registered the smell of cigarette smoke, which he didn't like, but it hadn't made him look up to see where it was coming from. Danny and Alan, both smoking, were just a few meters away.

"Hello, worthless," said Danny almost pleasantly as he and Alan approached the bench. "What are you doing here?"

"Nothing," replied Martin quietly, feeling queasy and nervously rolling the XP50 in his hands.

"Nothing," mocked Alan.

"What's that you've got?" Danny pointed at the XP50.

"Nothing," mumbled Martin again.

"Is that all you can fucking say?" spat Alan.

"It's just something I found."

"Oh well... finders' keepers, losers weepers," said Danny in a measured tone. "I found you with it, so it's mine to keep." His tone denoted impeccable logic.

"This is something that... which... I... it could be..." Martin stumbled over his words, not sure what he wanted to say.

"I really do think you should give it to me," Danny interrupted. His casual tone continued to distress Martin, especially as Alan was nodding his head slowly in mock emphatic agreement. "Otherwise," he paused, "losers weepers," he added in a different tone altogether.

Several months previously, Martin had watched a fight between Danny and Tommy Bradley on the school field. Tommy was the Year 12 equivalent of Danny, except that he was larger and even more unpleasant. A sizable crowd had gathered when it started. Like most real, uncontrolled violence, it didn't last long. Even so, by the time a teacher broke it up, Danny's face was red from the blows it had taken, and he was crying from the pain, although he was trying extremely hard not to show it. Tommy had blood pouring from his nose and had to be taken to hospital with what later turned out to be a dislocated shoulder.

Martin knew he was no Tommy Bradley, not even a thin, pale imitation of a shadow of Tommy Bradley. There was no chance of him inflicting any damage whatsoever on Danny in a fight, or of preventing him from getting whatever he wanted, even if Alan Lucas hadn't been there as well.

"What do we do, Alan?" asked Danny in mock puzzlement. "What... Do... We... Do?"

"We just take it," said Alan, who leaned forward and jabbed his cigarette into the top of Martin's right hand. This hurt a lot more than Martin ever thought such a thing would. He dropped the XP50 onto the grass.

He knew he was going to have to give it up. Whatever the XP50 was, he was going to have to hand it over, and he was also probably going to get hurt, even if he did.

Yet, against the odds, suddenly all the repressed and previously denied misery caused by Danny rose up inside him, and he suddenly saw Danny's actions over the past months for what they were. All the bullying and humiliation flashed through his mind. And so did a plan.

"Bloody have it then," he said. Martin felt good using a swear word – something he hardly ever did. It seemed to give him power. He kicked the XP50 so that it rolled under the bench. As Danny bent to pick it up, Martin pushed him aside – which also made him feel good – and ran. As hard and fast as he could.

He didn't think Danny or Alan would come after him, and when he turned after about 15 seconds, he had covered about 80 metres and could see that he was right. They'd sat down on the bench and were looking at what they'd taken from him.

Once again, several thoughts ran through his mind very quickly.

Firstly, and under the circumstances, he had no idea why it occurred to him, hadn't the designers of the XP50 ever thought that, in a battle, it might be hard to hear 'an audible click'?

Secondly, Danny wouldn't bother to get out his phone and look up what an XP50 actually was. Danny would assume, just as he had initially, that it was a thermos or maybe a spray can or something like that. He would simply unscrew the top and press the red button to see what happened.

Thirdly, the XP50 only worked about 50% of the time.

50% of the time; a flip of a coin.

Perhaps he'd get lucky.

Reflection

How does Martin's behaviour compare to how you would react if you had been in his situation?

Are there aspects of Martin's character that you would like to have known more about?

My Uncle Roy

My uncle Roy was fat. I know, I know; I shouldn't use that term, but bear with me. Actually, a lot of my relatives from my mother's side of the family were. Of course, we never used that word; 'big-boned' was the phrase used when we mentioned it at all, which was not often. But Uncle Roy, and the lady he married, my Aunt Joyce, along with my cousins Ellis and Mandy, were not just 'big-boned'; they also liked to eat. A lot.

Having said that, the one thing Aunt Joyce could be relied upon to say whenever we went to their house, or they all came over to ours, was that she was 'on a diet'. Maybe she was for that one day, but she can't have been for all the other days we weren't together. Or, if she was, it was the wrong sort of diet. Uncle Roy was even larger than her. So what? So bloody what? They were both genuinely lovely people who always had something kind and supportive to say to me right from my earliest days — from when they came round in December just before 'the big day' (when I still believed in Father Christmas) to when I was nervously about to go off to university.

I remember those family occasions very well; Uncle Roy was always laughing. He laughed at just about anything; it wasn't false, it wasn't forced, it wasn't embarrassing. It was just that he found humour in so many things. I never knew him to be 'down' — although, as you'll see, he obviously sometimes was. From my earliest years, I can recall him eating several helpings of everything at mealtimes, saying, "Mustn't let it go to waste!" Afterwards, he'd slap his hands over his enormous tummy and say, "Keeps you warm in winter!" and we'd all, always, laugh. He really was a nice man.

My mother, who came from the 'small-boned' side of her family, always talked about her brother in positive terms. She was very fond of him. "Your Uncle Roy is a lovely man. A very kind man. He'll stand up to anyone who's being horrid to someone else." As I got older, I wondered if that last statement referred to some incident involving her when she was younger, but I never asked her, and so I never got to find out. She might have varied the order of those statements over the years, but they were unwavering, and she always sounded like she meant what she was saying.

So, as a child, I knew how kind he was, and I also knew that he was very clever because my mum had told me, and you believe your mum, don't you? Whatever it was he did at work, and wherever it was, he was 'an important and clever man,' she said. I remember that statement clearly because it was odd that no one ever mentioned exactly what Uncle Roy did or where he worked. "He works for the government," I can remember Mum saying, but always with a slight tinge of uncertainty as to in what capacity that was. In later years, I realised that she didn't actually know.

I did ask him, once, where he worked when I was about twelve. He replied at once, "At the ministry down in London." That was the end of that because I didn't want to admit that I only had a vague notion of what a ministry was. I had an inkling there was more than one, but he'd definitely said 'the ministry.' I think I just tried to look as if he had satisfactorily answered my question.

Uncle Roy died eighteen months ago. Heart attack. Only 71. Aunt Joyce, also 71, died a week later, apparently of a stroke. Coincidence? I'm not going there.

When they died, my cousins Ellis and Mandy (who Ellis always affectionately referred to simply as 'M') did all the sorting out — the legal and the physical stuff. I knew what this involved from the death of my own parents; it's not easy. What do you give away to a charity shop, what do you simply throw away, and what, if anything, should you offer to any relatives?

It's this last issue that has resulted in what I'm writing now. Ellis knew I enjoyed science fiction, whereas he and Mandy didn't. Uncle Roy had a large collection of classic material; Isaac Asimov, Frank Herbert, E. E. 'Doc' Smith, Arthur C. Clarke, and loads of other stuff. I'd always find myself looking at his bookshelves enviously (there were some first editions there) when we visited, and I can recall asking him one time when I was about 16 who he thought the best writer of all was. I've never forgotten his reply because his tone implied, so it seemed to me at the time, that I was on the same cerebral level as him regarding such matters and so would understand his reasoning. He put his hand on my shoulder as we stood in front of the bookcase.

"Herbert wrote an unassailably brilliant, classic first book in *Dune* — the next two in the series are really good as well; he was a hell of a writer, but after those three... well, it all seems to lose its way. And I remember thinking, 'God knows what he was on about with the other books.' I haven't opened them for years. Clarke? Very astute. Prescient." (I had to look that word up.) "But in answer to your question, there's only one candidate; it's Asimov, and if you've read his stuff, you'll know why."

I told him that the *Foundation* material was my favourite, and he positively beamed as he nodded approvingly.

This is probably why Ellis asked me if I'd like to have his dad's old books. "I don't want them, neither does M, and Dad knew you were into them, so come over and help yourself. We'll be pleased to see them go to a good home."

So, I did go over. Ellis and Mandy had helpfully packed the books into various cardboard boxes, and I said something like, "Yes, great, I'll take these, are you sure?" Then I noticed in one of the boxes was a battered ring binder that was falling to pieces, with some of the pages loose and falling out. The cover simply had the words 'my notes' written on it.

A Different Approach and Other Stories

I asked what it was. Ellis didn't know, but Mandy answered that it was 'just some stuff Dad had written'. She said she'd 'only glanced at one page in the middle of it' and that what she'd read hadn't made any sense. She said she thought he was 'trying to do his own sci-fi stories', which was why she wanted me to have it.

And so we come to it. The rest of all this is about what Uncle Roy had written. Written, not typed. I've typed it, and I'm presenting it exactly as the pages were in that ring binder. After you've read it, maybe, like me, you'll think there are bits missing — lost years ago or perhaps recently in the reshuffle of everything after he died. Maybe he intended to put other bits in later or change the order of some of it. Who knows? That's all I'm going to say about it for now. It isn't something I can give you any sort of introduction to, although I've put my own thoughts in occasionally, in italics.

'The notes' were as follows:

For years, I've worked on something similar to the CIA's Project Star Gate. This was, or perhaps still is depending on who you believe, the CIA's psychic warfare program involving activities like scrying, remote viewing, telepathy, and mind control.

Well, I worked on a kind of UK programme of those sorts of activities. I don't know whether we contributed to the CIA's programme. Things at the ministry are very compartmentalised. Need-to-know basis, etc. What I finally ended up working on was perhaps, well, almost certainly is, even more unbelievable and weird.

(The writing continued straight into this next paragraph. Things sort of 'change tack' here and again in the paragraph afterwards, but there is nothing missing. This is how it appeared.)

A few years ago, I saw a recruitment advertisement on TV for teachers. It mentioned how teachers can 'help shape a life' or something similar. I remember it well because I remember that two of my teachers did just that; they shaped my life. The first one was an English teacher, Mister Coleman. He was from New York, and I have no idea why he was teaching in England. He was taking us through Shakespeare's *Hamlet.* He went on about a particular line that Hamlet said to his friend Horatio: "There are more things in heaven and earth than are dreamt of in your philosophy." We all looked a bit puzzled until Mister Coleman said that a modern translation could be: "There's a lot of crazy crap going on in the world that we don't know about or understand." I never forgot that comment. *(I had never heard Uncle Roy use any swear word, even a mild one, before, so this was a surprise, but he was only reporting what his teacher had said.)*

Einstein won a Nobel Prize. What a man. What a mind. I don't think anyone who isn't a physicist can really appreciate what that man did. To most people who know of him — and there is a disturbingly large number who don't — he was just 'very clever' in the way that all Nobel Prize winners must be. But it goes beyond that. Way beyond that.

I, or rather I should say the team I led, built on his work. Actually, I don't see why I should be modest, I did most of the work, although the others obviously helped. I've done something amazing with it.

(A new page started with)

No one is going to be foolish enough to call someone like me or Joyce 'fat' anymore. Ever. Here's why.

(I thought this was very odd and disjointed. Was there a page leading into this, missing here?)

It's all quite strange, really, because initially, I never paid much attention to physics at school because it was very complicated, at least to me, and our physics teachers in the early years were not very good with pupils like me. They were great with the 'high-fliers', but none of them had any time for those who struggled with the subject. Sink or swim. I was sinking. Now, the school insisted we take at least one science subject to exam level, and I chose Physics. I'm not sure why. I didn't like Chemistry either, and Biology was not so much incomprehensible as just plain boring, but I had to choose something.

Reluctantly, I chose Physics. Perhaps it really was 'more things than in my philosophy' guiding me. It turned out to have been the right thing to do. My new teacher was Mr Dollenby. He was totally different to any of the other physicists and started almost from scratch, which meant that pupils like me began to understand the subject. Not only 'understand', but 'get into'; I started to prefer it to all my other subjects, and I began to get very good at it.

This was when I was about fifteen. I can remember the lesson when all of what has followed in terms of my discoveries started. Mr Dollenby told us that back in the last century, Einstein had come up with a theory that explained how mass and energy are the same thing. I had always thought that 'mass' just meant a lump of something — and in a way, I was right. It basically does mean that; a lump of something is 'matter'. The point is that they are the same; they just exist in different forms and, under certain conditions, can be converted, changed if you prefer that word, into each other.

Mr Dollenby went on about how Einstein's theory said that the amount of energy possessed by something is equal to its mass multiplied by the square of the speed of light. $E=mc^2$. I'd heard that formula before, but until then, never knew what it meant.

I suddenly understood that it was possible for a lump of something to be changed into energy. Mr Dollenby explained that this is how nuclear power is generated and how nuclear bombs work. The mass gets converted to energy. But the conditions have to be right.

I was really into this idea.

I'm not going to go on about how nuclear bombs and power stations work; you can look that up yourself. *(I suddenly wondered if these notes had been written for Ellis and Mandy. Who else would Roy be telling to look it up?)* There are plenty of easy-to-understand clips on places like YouTube about how uranium and plutonium get changed into energy through the splitting of atoms. What is not there, and what is not explained, is how a human can convert part of his or her body mass into energy. That is what I've been working on. *(At this point, I wondered if this was the bit that Mandy had read.)*

After that lesson, I wondered if Einstein had spent years working towards the conclusion that energy was the same thing as mass, or whether he thought it was pretty obvious from the start but then had to spend ages working out the equations to prove it. With me, from that one lesson (this is going to sound very grand, but I don't care), a seed was planted in my mind about how a living being — not a piece of uranium or plutonium — might be able to use some of his or her mass to change it into energy. Don't ask me why, but I thought it might be possible right from that lesson.

Physics, and some other subjects, I liked, but I didn't always have a happy time at school. The reason why may well have influenced the path of my life just as much as the words of Mister Coleman and the approach of Mister Dollenby. *(This was all on a single sheet, and the bottom part of it was torn away, so there might have been something missing. The next sheet continued...)*

I remember my father once showing me a photo of his mother, who was called 'Lottie', as a young woman, that he'd found in an old box in the loft. *(Again, I wondered who he had written all of this for. If Ellis and Mandy, why not say 'your grandmother'?)* He was really pleased to find it because it was in good condition for its age, and also almost all the pictures of her had been lost when moving house in the past. He told me Lottie had worked in a carpet factory in between having four children. She looked like someone who could lift a massive roll of carpet single-handed without the slightest difficulty. I doubted if her supervisor ever tried to intimidate her, even back in the days when employees, especially females, were easily bullied. Big-boned? Yes. Very. I think I inherited a large share of her genes.

I have always been overweight. On the large side. I don't like other people saying I'm (or Joyce is) 'fat', but as I've said, people are soon going to be very reluctant to use that term. It could have nasty consequences for them. I got picked on a bit at school. I wouldn't say 'bullied' as such, but observations were sometimes made about my size.

Luckily, I could deflect many of the comments fairly easily. Telling rude jokes involving swear words, which were far in advance of my years, was one way. *(Really? Where did Uncle Roy get them from?)* After some remark was directed at me, I'd just say, in an exaggeratedly bored way, "Yes, yes. Ha ha. But have you heard the one about...?" I was able to handle it most of the time, but I wished I didn't have to. I really wished I didn't. So, childhood experiences definitely affected me later in life. Well, whoever you are, how could they not?

Anyway, I never forgot what Mister Dollenby taught me and how he inspired me. I took an 'A' level in physics, then a degree in it, then a doctorate, and then I ended up working for the ministry on various projects, of which this one about body mass into energy was the most interesting and important. It's taken me most of my working life. I've been lucky at work; the ministry had people who would actively encourage and persevere with these slightly (slightly?) crazy ideas, even when governments were trying to cut back on funding — and there are certainly other projects I can talk about *(I never found anything relating to these)*, but this one was the most important.

I did lose some weight by jogging (or 'running', as it was called in those days) in my twenties. And for a brief time, I even did some boxing. In fact, I quite enjoyed that. And the exercises I did there were later useful in my discovery.

It is all very well having imaginative ideas as a child, but where does the ability to try 'taking it forward' come from? Like I said, the ministry encouraged strange ideas, and I was always having them. The truth is that, in this case, I woke up one morning with some very odd but logical ideas and equations in my head.

The process doesn't need anything like the devices that trigger nuclear bombs *(I actually did go and look this up)*; it just needs the right mental, well, 'thoughts' isn't quite right, 'processes' is better — accompanied by some muscular contractions.

Who knows in sleep what dreams may come? Wasn't that another bit of Shakespeare? Who knows what thoughts may come and why when you are asleep. I suppose psychiatrists do. Perhaps that day I had been thinking back on some of the comments that had been made to me years ago back at school; I've never forgotten them. And there was someone at the ministry who always made remarks aloud about my weight. This was when such remarks were regarded as witty rather than offensive and before 'bullying at work' was taken seriously. *(I wondered how Uncle Roy dealt with him/her. The same way as he did at school?)* Or maybe my subconscious had been processing some of the concepts from university or even Mister Dollenby's lessons for years and suddenly decided 'now is the time'. But in all honesty, exactly how it all fell into place will always be a mystery to me.

All I know is that when I woke up, I had some very radical thoughts, ideas, and concepts in my head that I needed to write down as fast as possible. It seemed obvious to me what I might be able to do. Was this how Einstein had felt? I read somewhere that when he heard about Hiroshima, he said, "If I had only known, I would have been a locksmith." Well, the cat was rather obviously out of the bag by then, and anyway, didn't someone else say that technology is neutral? It can be used for good or bad. I'd like to think my discovery will be used for good, but doubtless, some will think of ways to abuse it. Luckily, the way it works isn't easy to master, and for some reason, those who can master it have all been, so far, on the large side like me.

The basics are simple: if you want to move an object, you have to apply a force to it. That needs some 'work', like a push. This means energy gets transferred to the object so it moves. That energy has to come from somewhere. The breakthrough I made was that I now knew how to convert some of my body mass into energy.

It isn't a nuclear explosion! I don't need uranium; I can do the work and push and change ordinary static air, which has mass, into wind, which has kinetic energy — the energy of motion. That motion could be a gentle trickle of a breeze, a strong jet of wind, or a single 'punching' blast. How much energy is created and how great the push depends on the mass I choose to use, or I suppose I should say 'lose'.

As you can imagine, it was all very hit or miss to start with. Nothing dramatic like smashing down a wall, but objects did get broken accidentally — well, shattered actually — and people did get knocked about a bit. It still works better close up than at a distance, but perfecting that will be for others. I started it and can still do it. There are others who took over when I retired two years ago and are more than capable of doing this. I hear, informally, they are making very good progress. An obvious point here is that larger people have more mass, and so they have more potential to turn that mass into energy.

The upshot of this is that there will come a day when 'fat' people are going to be feared. No one is going to know if they have, let's call it 'the technique'. Larger people are going to get the respect they deserve. The government 'owns' the idea, but I know already that two people I worked with have shared at least some of this information. *(I wondered if they hadn't signed the Official Secrets Act or something. There was also, of course, the possibility that even if they had, there was such a huge amount of money to be made it might have been tempting to break it — and who would believe this tale anyway at a trial? It is too fantastic an idea.)* It will get out and spread in the same way that nuclear technology did.

Incidents recently have shown... *(Try as I might, I couldn't read the next few words; it looked as though coffee or something had been spilled on the paper)* and I'm going to write down some... *(Again, the coffee or whatever obscured the last few words. And that was it. It obviously wasn't complete. Pages missing? Never finished it? Whatever, there was no more.)*

I called Mandy and asked her, "Is there any more of that story your dad started writing?" She said she didn't think so; that was all she and Ellis had found. She asked if it was any good. I said it was certainly strange and interesting, but very far-fetched. Yes, that was it. Well, at least as far as the notes went. Then, in something of a lightbulb moment a few days later, I suddenly realised what 'incidents recently' must be referring to. Uncle Roy had written this not long after he'd retired, which was when he was

66, so the 'incidents' would have been about seven years ago. I had been living and working in France at the time but remember my mother calling one day and giving me the shocking news that Uncle Roy had been charged with Grievous Bodily Harm after a fight outside a pub. Needless to say, at first, I thought it was some sort of joke, although even as I considered that remote possibility, I was thinking that Mum was never likely to say such a thing.

Recalling that incident now puts a very different perspective on things.

Like me, no one could believe that Uncle Roy was being tried for GBH. Uncle Roy. GBH. A man well into his sixties. But there was no doubt, and he didn't deny it, that he had been involved in 'an incident', and the Crown Prosecution Service thought there was sufficient evidence to charge him. That he had been provoked was not in doubt, but the case was based on his use of excessive force — very excessive force — in self-defence against someone called Micky Spier.

Mum and Dad went to the court almost every day to follow Uncle Roy's trial, and to support him, of course, against the GBH charge. Aunt Joyce was being called as a witness and so was not allowed to hear what others had said before her turn came. Mum called me every night with an update.

It had all happened outside a pub one evening. Uncle Roy and Joyce had met up with some old friends for a drink. On the night in question (as the saying goes), there had been an incident earlier in the evening when Roy and Spier accidentally bumped into each other in the pub. Both slightly spilled the drinks they were carrying. Uncle Roy, when giving evidence, said he wasn't particularly annoyed, even though he'd just bought the drinks. He regarded it as an accident, but Spier had been angry and had called him a clumsy fat wanker.

Uncle Roy stated that he hadn't responded, had walked away, and assumed the incident—unpleasant though it was—was over. When their friends left an hour or so later, he and Aunt Joyce decided to leave as well and went to catch the bus home. To the right of the pub was a clothes shop with a large plate-glass window, and the bus stop was opposite that.

While they were waiting for the bus, Spier and two of his friends came out of the pub to have a cigarette. Spier, seeing Uncle Roy and Aunt Joyce, decided to resurrect the earlier confrontation.

Mum said the CCTV from one of the pub's outside cameras showed it all quite clearly. Spier, on noticing Uncle Roy and Aunt Joyce, approached them and started having a go at them—aggressive finger-pointing and body language. Uncle Roy testified that the language used by Spier was similar to that which had been used previously. The comments to Aunt Joyce were not nice either, Mum said.

Uncle Roy was seen to say something, which he said in court was basically, "It was all an accident. Look, let it go, we're going home."

This didn't have the desired effect and, for some reason, worsened the situation. After further pointing and shouting, Spier pulled a knife from his jacket and moved towards Roy and Joyce.

The CCTV apparently showed this next stage very clearly as well. Uncle Roy then adopted what Mum said was 'a sort of karate stance', steadying his body while saying something. Spier still came at him. Roy stretched his right arm out, wriggled it slightly, and then extended it straight with palm up in the classic 'stop right there' position.

Spier didn't stop and continued to close in on him. The knife was very close to Roy, and Spier made a jabbing motion with it. Uncle Roy moved backwards quickly, avoiding the blade. It wasn't clear if Spier was just trying to intimidate him or whether he actually intended to stab him, but it was clearly a very nasty situation.

Then, Mum said that Uncle Roy flicked his hand down, up, then down again in what she described as a 'just go away' waving manner. Spier was, however, not waved away, but was seen (again, very clearly) on the CCTV to fly backwards onto and through the window of the clothes shop next to the pub.

As a result, he was very badly cut by the glass. The top of him went straight through it, but the back of his legs were impaled on the shards. He was very seriously injured and nearly died due to loss of blood.

Spier was charged with possession of a bladed article (aggravated, of course, by it being waved around and used to threaten). Uncle Roy's charge was that he had used more than reasonable force to defend himself. But of course, the central issue was: had Uncle Roy hit or pushed him at all?

Mum said they kept on and on playing the CCTV footage, but that no matter how many times it was played or at what speed, it showed that he had not. He'd adopted a fighting stance, put out his hand, and flicked it at Spier. But despite Spier's evidence, it was clear that he had at no time made contact with him.

Uncle Roy's defence barrister, presumably with his client's approval, asked the jury to consider the age and demeanour of the accused. He was hardly "the type of character usually seen in these courts charged with this offence," he had said. Mum said he was very eloquent. Well, barristers are, aren't they?

He wondered aloud, for the jury's benefit, why the charge had been brought at all given the nature of the evidence. He twice made the point that Spier must have realised how foolish his actions were, had thankfully decided to 'back off', had quickly stepped backwards and slipped or tripped, which resulted in his falling backwards onto and through the shop window.

Mum said that although her brother never touched Spier, that explanation wasn't how it appeared to her (and maybe the jury) on the CCTV.

Nevertheless, the jury didn't take long to reach a verdict. Uncle Roy was unanimously found not guilty.

Mum wasn't surprised. After all, as she said when she called me that night, what other explanation was there?

Reflection

To what extent is Uncle Roy's work and enthusiasm for his discovery motivated purely by revenge?

Be Careful
What You Wish For

I'm going to get this down quickly because I don't want to forget it. If it's rough and ready, so be it. There's no point polishing it up later because it is what it is—or was what it was. This is what I dreamed.

I can fly! I don't mean that I'd conquered a phobia about being on a plane, no—I mean I could actually fly. I just sort of glided up into the air with no problem and guided myself to where I wanted to go. I didn't flap my arms or do a Superman pose or anything—it was all graceful. And that's where the dream started: I flew out of a top-floor window of a house, then down to the garden. There was some sort of party going on down there. I don't know whose.

Someone, seeing what I'd done, said, "Can you change the bulb on the landing? It's impossible without a ladder." I nodded. We went inside. A bulb was handed to me, and I glided up and did it. I could fly.

Nobody else there could fly. Although I was enjoying people watching me, I wasn't smug or anything; I just did it—like an expert pinball player casually racking up points, or a brilliant guitarist noodling while only half concentrating.

Then a voice in my head said, *"But you're just dreaming."*

Yeah, well, I knew that already. But the voice, a male voice, then said, *"You know, you can swap to this existence if you want to."*

This confused me. "You mean I can come here?" I asked the voice (I couldn't see anyone). "To this place where I can fly?"

"Yes, the 'you' from where you can't fly can come here, where you can fly—and the 'you' who can fly here can swap to where you're dreaming from now. Where you can't fly."

"What do you mean 'the me that's here who can fly?'" I demanded. This all sounded like bollocks to me. But—there was something about it all that wasn't like a normal dream.

"Where you are now is a parallel universe—an alternate reality—and you can swap from your reality to this one."

"How is this possible? Why would I want to do it?" I asked.

The answers came back at once. *"Good questions. You really need to be thinking about this... A swap is only possible when both of you are dreaming simultaneously and thinking about doing a swap because you like where you are now and want to get away from where you normally exist. The 'flying you'—I mean, the one who can fly—is, by chance, currently dreaming and seeing your reality; the life that you usually lead. That's why I'm here—to possibly facilitate a swap. As for why you'd want to do it, that's up to you both."*

"What are you?" I asked. "How is this possible?"

"I've just told you. I'm a facilitator."

"An angel?"

"Oh no, no, no! Nothing like that. Or a demon—although if I was, I suppose I would say that, wouldn't I?" (The slightly musing tone as this was said suggested to me that he wasn't.) *"I'm just doing my job. It's possible to swap because there are different realities."*

"Doing your job? Who employs you?"

"Look," said the voice. *"I used the wrong phrase there. This is something that I do. But you—both of you—are not going to be asleep and dreaming for long. It doesn't matter to me what does or doesn't happen, but if you want it to happen, the swap, then you'll both have to make a decision soon. I'm saying exactly the same things right now to the 'able-to-fly' you who is currently looking at the situation—your life—where you come from."*

"Can I change back if I swap?" I asked.

"Technically, yes. But it isn't just a case of you saying, 'I don't want this anymore—I'd like to go back to the non-flying me.' And vice versa. You'd both have to be dreaming and both agree to swap back all over again. The chances of that are very, very small, as you can imagine."

"But this is just crazy," I said. "This is like going to a party and seeing someone you really like the look of… you have a quick chat and then decide to get married."

There was a pause. I thought I must have offended him. But no—quite the opposite.

"That's actually a good way of putting it. I'll remember that line. But swaps do happen on that basis. I'll give you an example. A real one. I suppose that might help."

"It might," I replied.

"OK. In one reality, there was someone who'd had most of his left leg amputated after a car accident. Someone swapped with him. Someone became that person with only one leg. You have to realise that there are different realities. Lots of them. Thousands of them. Millions of them. Not just the two that you and the flying you inhabit. When you 'dream' you are actually temporarily in another of those realities. Which one you go to is random—I have nothing to do with it. I'm just here if two dreams intersect. Well, someone swapped into the reality of that person who'd lost his leg."

I know what you are probably thinking reading this. I asked too—"Why?!"

"Well, the person who'd lost his left leg dreamed and found himself in a reality which gave 'him'—the him with two legs—a dreadful time. A lot of terror. There was this huge… oh well, I'll have to call it a 'monster'—sort of like a big dog with massive eyes and

big fangs—that kept appearing and terrifying him. Nothing he could do would stop it. It had been going on all his life. In that reality, that sort of thing happened to people. Monsters followed them."

You see, realities are very, very different. Anyway, the one-legged man enters that reality and sees the monster. The monster tries its usual tricks, and the one-legged bloke goes, "Oh, you don't scare me. I bet you're quite friendly really," or something like that. The monster growls a bit, but the bloke repeats something similar. The monster eventually 'gives in' and actually is friendly—and you won't believe this—furthermore, the man's partner in this 'monster world' was actually the one-legged man's old girlfriend from school thirty years ago in his reality.

Now, our one-legged friend had always wondered what had happened to her. So, he gets the chance to have both legs again, he's made a friend of this monster, got rid of its terror, and he's met up with the love of his life from all those years ago. So, he's up for a swap. You follow?"

"I think so," I said, albeit hesitantly.

"Right. Good. Now meanwhile, two-legs hated the monster so much that he'd do anything to avoid it. His life in that reality was ruined. He was a wreck. He'd never found a way to get rid of it. When he was in one-leg's reality, there was no monster and he got on well with one-leg's partner. He wasn't getting on all that well with his old school partner in his 'monster' reality. So, for him, it *was better to have one leg rather than two—escape something that had been terrorising him, and also get out of a failing relationship."*

"This is too weird," I said. "Monsters making everyone's life a misery. People in that reality can't do anything, but the one-legged man can? Come on! How does that work?"

"I don't know," said the voice, sounding slightly affronted. *"Not my part of the ship. I'm not an expert on what goes on in different realities."*

A tangential thought struck me. "Can this happen to children?"

"I get asked that from time to time," came the response. *"The answer should be 'no' because kids don't have the life experience to know what they actually want. It's a bit like..."* (there was a pause) *"...you shouldn't buy and drink alcohol until you are eighteen. But...."* Another pause.

"But kids still find a way to drink?" I prompted.

"Kids still find a way to drink."

Suddenly, a long-buried memory became clearer and clearer. There was someone I was friends with at school in Year 9—Tim Brock. I used to go round to Tim's house; we went out riding our bikes, we played football and stuff. At the end of that year, I didn't see him at all over the summer holiday for some reason.

When we went back in Year Ten, he'd totally changed. He'd become an aggressive bully; picked on the weaker lads and started challenging the pecking order of the year group. At break and lunchtime, he went for the traditional 'smoke behind the bike sheds'. Rude to the teachers too. We remained on vague 'nodding terms' but things were never the same. No more football or bike riding.

There's more: he met a girl—Jane, her name was—and he scratched 'Jane' into his arm with a compass point until it bled and then put black ink on it. He showed me; it looked awful, very naff—but obviously I wasn't going to say anything. My mate Tim had gone; replaced by someone else. I remember that I kept thinking, *What happened?* He got expelled eventually for spitting at one of the ladies serving in the dining hall when she told him not to push in front of the younger kids.

Was that down to this? Had he swapped? If so, why?

"Will you do this job forever?" I asked, suddenly following a different train of thought. I'm not sure why.

"Forever is a long time."

"Do you die?" (I'm not sure why I asked that either.)

"Not like you think of it, but I'm not going to talk about that because we have very limited time. Both of you seem to be considering the possibility of a swap. Do you want to take it? Like I said, it won't make any difference to me. Oh, and by the way, you won't remember this conversation when you wake up. Wherever you wake up."

"If I swapped, would I remember the 'me' that I was before?"

"If you've ever had an operation, the surgeon would have told you that there are risks associated with it. Yes?"

I'd had a growth on my vocal cords removed so I knew what he meant, and said so—though I didn't immediately understand why that question had been asked.

"That risk is usually presented as small—which it normally is—but it's there. Same here. You shouldn't remember the other 'you', but it does happen about one percent of the time. And when it does happen, as you can appreciate, there can be mental problems depending on how much you remember."

"Should I do it?"

"I'm not here to advise. I'm not allowed to advise. Now look, you're almost out of time."

"Well, I can fly and that was really nice. Others couldn't. But I don't know anything about anything else in this reality. I can't do this. Like I said... seeing someone at a party and all that."

"No problem. But I had to ask. That's why I'm here."

"Where's 'here'?"

"No time. The other you has decided he doesn't want to swap either—although he was closer to going for it than you. Anyway, I have to go. Others to deal with. As I already said, you won't recall any of this when you wake up. Bye."

But I *did* recall it, and I've written it down as best as I can.

Strangely, I've increasingly been thinking that things aren't right in my life—*all sorts* of things—and that I should really be doing other stuff somewhere else, in another place.

This is probably a coincidence. And I suppose it's just the way things are

Reflection:

Are dreams a prompt to action, a warning, both, or neither?'

The Startling Conclusions That Were Reached After the First Day's Questioning

The room was panelled with ancient oak and lined with oil paintings of long-dead members of the nobility who had once inhabited the house. There was a massive stone fireplace, nearly two metres wide, in the middle of one wall. The room had large windows that looked out over a huge, well-kept lawn, which had a lake at the far end. Tall trees with substantial trunks, obviously many years old, stood majestically on either side of the lawn. It all looked very much like the ground floor of some sort of eighteenth-century duke's stately home.

Which is what it was.

Or rather, what it once had been.

The furniture filling the room was starkly modern, with minimalist tables and chairs, a large monitor, computers, and various other pieces of electronic equipment that were distinctly at odds with their surroundings. The two soldiers standing next to the room's only door—each armed with a Heckler & Koch MP7—were clearly not part of any attempt at historical recreation either.

"Welcome, ladies, to your new accommodation. This is one of our conference rooms. We'll probably be spending quite a lot of time in here to start with. You'll be shown around properly later so that you can get acquainted with the place. You are going to be here for quite a while."

The woman who spoke these words to Suzie Cheng and Alice Marshall was tall, athletic, and very sharply dressed in grey. She had the appearance of someone who was used to being obeyed.

"Please, sit down," she continued, indicating the chairs surrounding the table in the middle of the room. The three of them sat.

"And you are?" demanded Suzie, lounging back in her seat.

"I am a major in the British Army. Major Lydia Porter. You can call me that if you like, or 'Major Porter', or simply 'Lydia' if you prefer. I don't mind. This lady"—she indicated a similarly sharply dressed woman, in blue rather than grey, who was already seated at the table as they entered—"is an American colleague of mine."

"My name is Courtney," the American stated, in an accent from one of the southern states. "Don't bother with the wiseass comment about us two being 'the women not dressed in black' because we've heard it before. I work for the FBI, not some weird organisation."

"FBI's weird enough," retorted Suzie.

"Heard that one before as well," replied Courtney, in a resigned rather than angry tone. She shot a look at Porter and a glance was exchanged. They had read about Suzie's ADHD.

Suzie looked disoriented but defiant. Alice was definitely the one most ill at ease.

"We recorded as much as we could. Should be worth millions when we sell it. We can sell some of it to you. Make us a proper offer and we'll accept," Alice said, with a slightly desperate edge to her voice.

"I'm afraid that isn't going to be possible," said Major Porter blandly—almost sadly.

"You're going to kill us?" stuttered Alice.

"Certainly not," replied Porter, looking rather affronted. "You're both much too valuable and"—her voice hardened almost imperceptibly—"as long as you accept the proposed..." (she paused slightly) "...arrangement, you will be very well paid and looked after. Employing hackers isn't a new idea, and it is a lot more common with businesses and governments than you might think. We need the best on our side. You have a very bright future—if you comply."

Suzie and Alice looked at each other but didn't speak.

"You did the impossible," continued Porter. "The British Army has one of the most powerful communication, information, and surveillance systems in the world—and you two hacked it. Twice."

(Suzie noticed that there was an almost imperceptible simultaneous grimace and slight roll of the eyes from Courtney at this point.)

"Furthermore, you got into Section 221B—which is why I'm here. 221B is now my area. It's my responsibility. A large number of people are not happy about what you did. Not. At. All." (These last three words were delivered with a pause, emphasising each one.)

"You got in once without alerting anyone. The second time, you accessed and used highly classified technology and then, before anyone was alerted, you managed to do something no one ever thought might be possible—in such a short period of time, or maybe even ever.

"You know what you did, and I'm sure you both realise why we want to know everything—*everything*—about what happened."

"And then?" asked Alice.

"Then it's likely we will offer you a very well-paid job—if you comply with our proposal. I've said that once."

"And if we don't comply?"

Alice thought the response to this question was going to be along the lines of a smooth-talking James Bond villain, full of underlying menace.

She couldn't have been more wrong.

"You have everything to gain from complying," said Porter. "No lifetime of routine jobs for you. No more doing what you obviously enjoy—hacking—only in your spare time. Your hobby will become your work. You'll join a team working—legally—with very sophisticated equipment. There are others like you who've joined us in similar circumstances, although none of them arrived with quite your pedigree."

"Working doing what?" asked Alice.

"Haven't you got it yet?" broke in Courtney, impatiently. "You're being offered the chance to hack other countries' systems—and protect yours. And mine. You don't get punished for what you did—you get rewarded."

"Perhaps you don't realise exactly the situation you are facing," said Porter, in a tone that implied it was actually impossible *not* to. "By which I mean the law relating to the hacking of computer systems. The legislation has a section—3ZA—which relates to unauthorised acts causing, or creating a risk of, serious damage. It is punishable by up to life in prison."

"It wasn't a cyber-attack; we didn't aim to sabotage anything. You know that. You know we never asked for a ransom. Nothing like that. And 'up to life in prison' doesn't mean we'd get that," said Suzie, all in a rush, using the same tone as before. She gave an exaggerated, sarcastic smile, crossed her arms, and stared pointedly at the ceiling.

Alice, however, wasn't looking so confident.

Porter noted this, ignored Suzie, and continued.

"You hacked a military system twice—utterly reckless of the consequences. You were caught red-handed. Who knows what your true aim was? Who knows what you intended to do with the information and data that you discovered? Who knows who you might have decided to sell it to? Or maybe you were just going to post it online for fun so it'd be available to anyone, any country, any terrorist, within minutes.

"I think I can take an informed guess as to how any judge is likely to regard your action—sorry, actions, plural—when you are found guilty. Go on, think about the likely outcome. It probably won't take you very long." She mouthed 'one, two, three' in a silent but exaggerated manner while slowly releasing the thumb and adjacent two fingers from the closed fist of her left hand.

The American then added, "And if it's discovered that what you did had any implications—any implications whatsoever—for my country's security the British Army has links with our comms, after all, then we'll want a piece of you when you're through with whatever prison time you've done here."

"I think they get the picture now, Courtney," Porter said.

"I hope so, for chrissakes," stated the FBI agent forcefully. "They are in deep, deep shit if they don't."

There was silence in the room.

Alice couldn't catch Suzie's eye, as she was still pointedly staring at the ceiling. She was fast forming the impression that this wasn't simply a 'good cop/bad cop' routine, and that their best hope—for whatever the future held—was, indeed, to trust Porter.

"How do we know we can trust you?" she nevertheless asked.

"You don't. But think about it. Your skillset is rather valuable. We'd very much like you on board."

"You mean in the tent pissing out rather than outside pissing in?" asked Suzie, still staring at the ceiling.

"Exactly," Porter replied. "Look, I can—and will soon—introduce you to some others working here who, as I said, joined us in the same sort of way as you. I know, I know..." (here she raised both hands in a submissive 'obviously you can't be certain it's genuine' manner). "But they will know a lot of the things that you know, and about what you did. They'll also, no doubt, want to know how you did it. You'll talk the same language. You'll recognise a fellow hacking enthusiast. But yes, it could still all be a sham with some well-trained actors, couldn't it?"

"And if we don't?"

"After all I've said? I really don't think that is going to happen. But OK—if you don't see reason, if necessary, you can be detained more or less indefinitely under some legislation that very few are aware of. And it won't be here..." (she gestured towards the window, towards the neatly manicured lawns), "...it'd be somewhere different. Very different."

"People will miss us; they'll wonder where we are," stated Alice.

"I don't think so, Alice. Neither of you have living parents. You have no brothers or sisters. Suzie has one brother, who she very rarely speaks to, and you are her only really close friend." (Suzie ceased looking at the ceiling and glared at her.) "I don't say that in an unpleasant way, I'm just stating a fact," Porter added, seeing the look she was getting. "Neither of you are in regular work. Your relationship, Alice, with Mark—is over, if you're honest. He's been in America for over two months..."

"Columbus, Ohio, to be precise," added Courtney.

"What, how...?" Alice stuttered.

"And he hasn't phoned you once—unless you have another phone that we don't know about, which is unlikely. No one is going to come looking for you."

Suzie and Alice looked at each other. They didn't need to speak. It was clear to both of them that they had no choice but to accept the situation.

"We'll go along with you—for now," Alice said, trying to add some significance to the final two words. It wasn't very convincing.

"Yeah. For now," sneered Suzie—even less successfully.

"Excellent," Porter replied—and sounded as if she actually meant it.

"Good choice," added Courtney. "Just don't forget the three magic words here: 'deep', 'deep' and 'shit'."

"There's others watching us now, isn't there?" said Suzie.

"Ooh, smart cookie," said Courtney, in an unnecessarily sarcastic tone.

"Of course there are. But who they are needn't bother you. There are also people looking at your computers right now—and your cloud storage," said Porter.

"You'll find those are..." began Alice.

"Incredibly easy to get into by someone with a talent similar to yours," interrupted Porter. "And as I've said, we have several of them."

There was another—this time longer—silence.

"Where do you want us to start?" asked Alice.

"We need to know everything. *Everything*," emphasised Porter. "You will be asked many things, many times, by many different people. It's going to take quite some time. It'll all take place here. Nice, isn't it? So much better than a police cell or a prison."

"Where's here?" demanded Suzie.

"Oh, somewhere secure. And private. With very nice facilities for you. I'll be the first to interview you. And naturally, when others do that, I'll always be around to look out for the welfare of my new employees."

"We haven't agreed to that," said Alice.

"Oh, please," Courtney said, using her sarcastic tone again.

Porter said nothing—but her expression clearly said, *Courtney's right*.

"I want some coffee," said Suzie.

"You and me both," replied Courtney.

"I'll organise it right away," said Porter pleasantly, reaching for a nearby phone. "Then we can get started. You are going to be interviewed separately, of course. Alice first, I think."

Alice's initial interview was not just with Porter; there were others—two men whose names and functions were not disclosed. They never spoke. Courtney was present too. Alice rightly guessed that the cameras in the room would be broadcasting to others as well.

The interview was very carefully conducted by Porter, who was exceedingly skilled at this type of conversation and kept the situation almost informal. She knew precisely what she wanted to find out and understood it couldn't all be done at once. There were probing questions, but never delivered in an aggressive manner. Porter didn't mind when Alice meandered back and forth—those in this sort of situation often did. Alice herself was, much to her surprise, almost—*almost*—at ease. Coffee was available as promised. And biscuits.

Unsurprisingly, some of the information extracted from Alice was already well known, but other elements were not. The most significant part of the first day's interview occurred in the final few minutes, where Alice—who had been allowed to talk extensively about her life in general—was finally prompted by Porter to begin describing the hacking process itself.

"Actually, 221B was the only area we got into. Your containment system worked. We tried other parts, but they were all too well protected. We got into 221B, though, the very first time we hacked the system. I can still remember Suzie's comment: '221B. Sherlock Holmes. Someone who solves complex and strange problems. Who the hell thought that was a good name? It's got me interested.' That's what she said."

"I don't think whoever named it was ever expecting it to be discovered and hacked," replied Porter mildly.

"Well, as Suzie said—and I agreed—it was bound to attract immediate attention if it ever was."

One of the men began tapping furiously on a tablet.

"If you've got any more with titles like that, I'd change them."

"A good point," replied Porter, who was obviously pleased with Alice's comment. "Not that we expect to be hacked again—which is where you'll be helping us. Why did you do it?" she continued in an almost casual manner. This was a crucial question, and one that would be asked of Alice and Suzie time and time again over the coming days.

Alice shrugged her shoulders and wrinkled her face in an 'I dunno' way. The clip of that expression would shortly be very carefully and repeatedly examined by experts in body language.

"We were bored. It was a new challenge—just a game," she said, in a tone that Porter, and all of those watching elsewhere, hoped they recognised as genuine. There was a collective sigh of relief from several of them—although Porter and the others in the interview room remained impassive.

"Then when it all happened, as we'd already been into 221B, we thought we'd try again and actually make use of what we'd found. We'd be famous. It was like this was all meant to be. We were very excited."

"I'm sure you were," said Porter, who was again pleased at the childlike naivety Alice was displaying. (This could be faked, of course, but she was hopeful it wasn't.) "It certainly did cause a lot of excitement. OK. Thank you for what you've told us. I need to speak to a few people now about what you've said. Let's take a break."

***

The alien spaceship had come out of nowhere. Literally nowhere.

NASA's SETI (Search for Extra-Terrestrial Intelligence) sites did not pick it up until it suddenly appeared just above Earth's exosphere, promptly alerting not only SETI but every other device on the planet capable of detecting it. The proverbial alarm bells started ringing across the globe.

It then seemed to 'dance' or 'wobble' for a few seconds—"as if deciding where to go next" (as one commentator later put it)—then headed earthwards in a flash, neatly avoiding all the communications satellites and space debris in its vicinity.

As a result of this, the laws of physics were declared by many to be in some need of modification. In short, it was almost impossible for the aliens to reach Earth unseen and appear in the way that they did.

Additionally, the nearest planet with conditions similar to Earth's was Proxima Centauri, some 4.2 light years away. That meant even if the aliens had come from there in a ship travelling at the speed of light, it would have taken them over four years to get here. If they were using a conventional Earth-produced rocket, it would have taken tens of thousands of years.

Even in the case of the former, how did they eat, drink, and breathe all that time (if they did)? And of course, they could have come from much, much further away. It was preposterous—and naturally, many refused to accept the visit was real. But it was.

There was no time for any country to 'scramble defences' or put 'missiles on standby' due to the nature and speed of its appearance. The alien spacecraft was not so much a 'gleaming flying saucer' as a greyish 'flying cake tin'—approximately twenty metres in diameter and ten metres high.

It landed on the lawn of Buckingham Palace in London.

This caused conflicting emotions in the governments of the world's global 'players'. On the one hand, if the aliens were hostile, it would be useful to see what happened in England first so that some sort of response—be it defence or attack (or both)—could be implemented. On the other hand, if the aliens turned out to be friendly, there was a huge propaganda gain to be had—and it wasn't them that were going to have it.

There were frantic demands from those concerned with royal security that the King—who was in residence (the Queen was not)—should be evacuated at once. But that didn't happen, although this wasn't widely known at the time.

An unnamed source later confirmed that King Charles responded rather forcefully to these demands along the lines of: "Out of all the places in the world, they landed in my bloody garden. I'm not going anywhere. Perhaps they want to meet me. *Me*, the King."

Although he refused to leave the palace, it is thought likely that he watched the proceedings remotely from the nuclear shelter beneath it.

Whether the aliens wanted to meet him or not, they certainly took no aggressive action. In fact, there was no action at all. The 'cake tin' simply hovered about a metre above the lawn. It stayed there for eighteen hours, thirty-four minutes and nine seconds before "silently zooming upwards into the sky and disappearing," as BBC News reported it.

Even less well known than the King's refusal to be evacuated was the fact that Suzie Cheng and Alice Marshall were the only two humans on the planet to communicate with the aliens during their visit.

***

"Well, you know the first part about them landing," said Suzie, not even waiting for a question.

Porter nodded; within a couple of hours of the aliens appearing, almost the whole planet did.

At school, Suzie's teachers used to say that she was "on the spectrum" – and in private added, "way off it." She had always been hyperactive, impulsive, and had trouble concentrating. Nothing had changed as she got older. Unless she was engaged in hacking – and even then, these traits didn't disappear altogether.

She had managed, with considerable difficulty, to gain a degree in software engineering, where she amazed and frustrated (mostly the latter) her lecturers. Since that time, two years ago, she had been unable to hold down a permanent job of any sort, existing on occasional freelance software design work.

Porter knew all of this and stared thoughtfully at Suzie, who was wearing a T-shirt with the single word *nightmare* on it. As well as the two silent and anonymous males who had been present with Alice, Courtney was there too. Porter knew that this initial interview could easily crash and burn with someone like Suzie. She decided to open with flattery.

"You two made contact with aliens. You actually communicated with them." She didn't risk antagonising Suzie by once again mentioning that this had been achieved illegally.

"First girls on the planet to do so. Woo hoo!" came the response.

"You succeeded where others couldn't."

"Didn't your lot try?"

"They did. So did others. And I'll be honest with you here, because I want you to be honest with me. They wouldn't answer because they were already talking to you. We think it might be that your communication was taken as... the Earth's official one, if I can put it like that, and so they jammed attempts by anyone else to—"

Suzie interrupted, giggling. "You mean they thought we were the rulers of Earth and wouldn't let anyone else try?!"

"That's exactly what I mean. Which is why I want you to be honest about what you communicated with them. I'd like to know exactly what you said, exactly what you did, exactly what you asked, exactly what you saw, and exactly what they said." Again, she didn't add the obvious; that these issues were uppermost in the minds of all of the world's leaders.

Suzie thought for a moment and then spoke in a rush.

"Well, we'd hacked your system on the Tuesday. Didn't tell anyone."

Porter looked pointedly at the camera as if to say *check the body language and tone* – although there was no need to do so, since some of those watching were already doing exactly that.

"The 221B thing, right? We now knew what it was for – the means of trying to talk to aliens. We could see how it would work.

"And then aliens arrived! The very day after! I mean really... We couldn't believe our luck. We could use the 221B system, we could get in first using it. At least we hoped we could. And we did – because you were a bit too slow. And because you were, we got in first!

"Now I saw that film *Arrival* some years ago – well, Ali had too – and in it they did like, teaching a child. You know, like basic principles of mathematics like πr^2, which the aliens knew about, to symbols and what they mean. Basic words to describe people and actions, all the while assuming they would understand them. We did that and they did too – or at least, maybe, well probably, their computers must have helped them, but they got it.

"Probably because they'd been here before – I'll tell you about that... They probably had some idea of what they were dealing with. Ali reckoned that too.

"We spent nearly eighteen hours non-stop. We must have drunk a gallon of black coffee. Then they stopped and flew away."

"You are obviously very clever, and we want others to benefit from that."

Suzie looked warily pleased with this comment, and so Porter decided to push ahead with the questioning. However, before she could start, Suzie spoke again.

"All this was recorded, you know. Of course you know. It's on our computers."

"I do know, but I want to hear it first from you. The recording won't tell me what you were thinking."

"We wanted to convince them that we were sentient and friendly."

"That was a good thing. A sensible thing."

"Not everyone, obviously. The planet is full of idiots. But you know, just that we were friendly."

"When you say 'we', you mean you and Alice?"

"Yeah, that was the first step. Get them to trust us. It worked. They told us lots of stuff."

"Like what?"

"It's all there. Recorded." Suzie suddenly sounded bored.

"Well, just give me the highlights of what you achieved."

"We sort of alternated our questions. Typing them. Ali and me. We never actually spoke. You know that, don't you?" (Porter nodded.) "It was all on-screen. We had loads to ask."

"I'm sure you did. And I'd very much like to know what you asked. And how they responded."

Suzie swallowed the last of her coffee and grimaced at the cup, as if wondering why she had bothered to do so.

"I can remember the first proper question, but after that, I can't remember the exact order of it all. Or all of it. It was eighteen hours anyway…"

"I don't mind the order," said Porter. "Just tell me what you remember saying, what you thought, and what you saw."

"First question was obviously 'Why are you here?' Look, can I tell this like question and answer?"

"Certainly. Whatever suits you best. I'm fascinated."

Which, whatever Porter's professional interests, was certainly true.

"Right, we asked – I mean I asked first, not Ali – and it went like this. Something like this; it wasn't like we were speaking, I mean typing and receiving perfect English."

Porter nodded encouragingly. Suzie became animated but focused. A rare event, Porter thought to herself.

'Have you been here before?'

'Yes, one time but you do not see us.'

'Why can we see you this time?'

'Hiding machinery failed.'

So, all that technology in *Star Trek* about cloaking devices actually exists, thought Porter.

'Why are you here?'

'Had to stop.'

'I mean, why do you visit our planet?'

'Passing by. See progress.'

'Progress towards what?'

'Evolution. Friendship. How you live.'

"Now I wanted to ask, 'how are we doing?' but Ali jumped in and randomly typed, 'How many of you are there in the spaceship?'"

"What was their answer?" asked Porter.

"Sixty-one," they said.

"So she then asks, 'Are you coming out to speak to us?' Or perhaps she said 'see us'. They go, 'No bugs'. Ali didn't get that. No bugs? No bugs? Like... what? Suddenly I got it. Not 'no bugs' – it's 'No. Full stop. Bugs.' They meant germs. Didn't want to catch anything from us – and vice versa. Sensible."

Porter nodded.

"So I go, 'Are we similar? Do you look like us and do we look like you?' They go, 'Yes and no.' We ran into a problem then because the answer to our question 'Explain' just generated words like 'size', 'move' and 'shape'. Well, I'm guessing they meant they were small – they must be if there were sixty-one on the ship. And I reckon if they understood pi, they could certainly count OK. As for 'shape' – we got nowhere with that either."

"Uh huh," said Porter encouragingly, who had a considerable number of specific questions to ask but thought it best to allow the stream of consciousness to continue.

"So Ali, who's a bit weird with this sort of stuff, just jumps in again and goes, 'Can we ask about your beliefs about life after death? We do not wish to offend you.'

"They go, 'You may ask.'

Ali goes, 'What is your belief?'

'About what?'

'What occurs when you cease to exist?'

'We do not cease to exist.'

'You are not immortal, are you?'

'No species are.'

'What is your belief then?'

'Belief?'

"What do you believe happens to you when you cease to exist in physical form?' OK, they might not have a physical form, but I just reckoned they did."

'Believe?'

"This was getting tricky, so I said to Ali, let's not push this. I go, 'Ali, you ever heard the phrase "when talking to someone you don't know, never talk about politics or religion"?'

"She goes, 'Don't you see that by saying "believe?" as a question it implies they know what happens after death, and that by asking them we've hopefully convinced them humans are definitely sentient?' Now me, I reckon they must obviously have known that already from the previous visit."

"Yes, but possibly not to that extent. Interesting," said Porter. "Now, my next question is very important – how did you convince them we are friendly? By which I mean you—or rather, we—had no intention of automatically attacking them as aliens. Did they ever intimate they..."

"Had weapons? Yeah, that's on the recording. I can't remember exactly what we said. Maybe something about, 'Are you worried about just turning up and causing conflict?' We didn't use the word 'war'. What they said was something like 'We are protected.' And Ali and I were thinking, as their technology is obviously better than ours, then they could attack us and defend themselves easily if they wanted to.

"They seemed interested in learning from us how the world was run and then got—well, I suppose 'puzzled' is the word—when we explained, or tried to, that different countries had different ways of ruling people. We asked why they wanted to know. They said 'Progress' again, I think.

"They also told us they were 'learning'. They suddenly brought up—and we hadn't said anything—people being sick, ill I mean, and underfed. 'No houses no food' they kept asking, by which I think they meant..."

"No houses and no food—question mark. Why don't these people have anywhere to live and enough to eat?" asked Porter.

"That's what we thought. Then it got a bit weird. For about two minutes there was actually some audio. There was a sort of, I suppose, clicking or clucking noise which I think was them speaking to each other, but it kept being interrupted by a sort of stuttering high-pitched squeal. Very weird."

"Let's return to the possibility of conflict," said Porter. "Did you ever consider that there could have been very considerable potential for something to happen if you said something offensive by mistake? I'm glad you didn't use the word 'small' to them, but you couldn't possibly know what words or concepts might be misconstrued. I think that crossed a lot of people's minds once they found out what you'd done."

"Fuckin' A," broke in Courtney.

Porter resumed, "For a few hours the whole planet was literally in your hands via what you two typed. Didn't you think about that?"

"Nah," replied Suzie, who had started to sound bored again.

"And why do you say that?"

"We showed them our cat," said Suzie promptly.

Courtney broke in again at this point with a voice sounding like something between a scream and a splutter. "You did what?! A cat!

A fucking cat! You showed them your cat? And how do you know they wouldn't interpret a cat as a threat of some sort?"

"Would you?" responded Suzie. And before Courtney could respond, added, "Actually, Domino showed himself to them. Jumped up on the desk in front of the camera as we were talking."

"Jesus H Christ," was all Courtney was now capable of saying.

"He's called Domino because he's a black and white cat," added Suzie helpfully. "Actually, he's a kitten. They were very impressed by the notion of a pet – it took nearly five minutes to explain."

It was thought appropriate to have a comfort break at that point.

Porter and Courtney walked outside the building. Neither said anything for a few moments. Courtney, whose body language implied she would have had no hesitation in single-handedly standing up to an advancing tank, lit a cigarette, and Porter moved so as to be upwind of the smoke.

"So, Courtney, what have we learned from these first interviews? Others are going to present their interpretation, but what summary do we report up the chain?"

It took several long moments for Courtney to bring herself under control. She took a deep drag on her cigarette, let the smoke out in a slow stream, and then asked, "Which of us is going to candidly report that Earth might have been spared from a devastating attack because of a pet cat?"

Porter didn't answer.

"And the clicking and clucking. You know what I think that was? Laughter! Laughing at the way we organise things on the planet. What the fuck. Why were they laughing?"

Porter, whose politics were more to the left than Courtney's, thought she knew the answer but didn't answer that question either.

Reflection

What do you think happens to Alice and Suzie when the questioning finally finishes?

What was the most memorable scene in the story and why?

Printed in Dunstable, United Kingdom